airy D s

Gwyneth Rees

Illustrated by Emily Bannister

MACMILLAN CHILDREN'S BOOKS

First published 2005 by Macmillan Children's Books

This edition published 2016 by Macmillan Children's Books
an imprint of Pan Macmillan
20 New Wharf Road, London N1 9RR
Associated companies throughout the world
www.panmacmillan.com

ISBN 978-1-5098-1866-2

1 3 5 7 9 8 6 4 2

A CIP catalogue record for this book is available from
the British Library.

Printed and bound by CPI Group (UK) Ltd, Croydon CR0 4YY

For my grandma, Hester Ivy Dawson,
with much love

1

Evie had always thought that fairies, if they lived anywhere, lived at the bottom of your garden. That's what her grandmother had always told her and today, when Evie mentioned throwing out her old doll's house, Grandma immediately suggested that she bring it over on her next visit so they could set it up at the bottom of the garden for the fairies to play in.

'Fairies are just like little girls,' Grandma told her. 'They like to play at houses and doctors-and-nurses and things like that.'

'How do you know?' Evie asked. She had never seen a fairy herself and her mother had always told her that there was no such thing whenever she'd asked her about them.

'I once saw two fairies down by the bottom flower bed. One was lying down and crying out that her wing was hurting, and when I went over to speak to her to see if I could help, she sat up and beamed at me and said not to worry because they were just playing. She was the patient and her friend was the nurse. The nurse one was bandaging up her wing with a white petal that had fallen from one of the flowers.'

Evie loved to hear her grandmother talk about the fairies, but she had learned a long time ago that she must never mention Grandma's stories to her mother. For some reason Mum got very cross whenever fairies were mentioned and she always told Grandma off if she caught her telling Evie about them.

So Evie was glad that her mother wasn't with them today as she went for a walk with Grandma to the church near her grandmother's house. It was the summer holidays and Evie and her mum had been staying with Grandma for the past week. It took three hours for them to drive to where Grandma lived, and Mum had asked her mother more than once if she'd like to come and live nearer to them, but Grandma had always refused. She was fiercely independent and very fit for an old lady because she went for walks in the countryside every day. She didn't want to leave her home and all her friends who lived in the same village as she did.

It wasn't a Sunday so the church itself was closed, but Grandma wanted to show Evie a special gravestone that she often talked about.

'We used to call her the white lady,' she explained as they reached the gates of the

graveyard. 'When I was a little girl I used to come here with my friends to look at her.'

Grandma had lived in the area all her life and had attended this church when she was young. Now the church had houses around it and a car park next to it, but Evie knew that when Grandma was a girl the church had stood on its own in the middle of the fields and you'd had to walk across the fields to get to it – unless you'd had a horse and then you might have ridden.

Grandma led Evie round a path to the back of the church and down into the oldest part of the graveyard, which was less well tended and very overgrown around some of the gravestones.

'There she is!' Grandma said, pointing to a very old, very dirty marble statue of an angel which must once have been white. One of her arms had broken off and her left wing was cracked. 'We used to come to see her after church every Sunday.'

'Whose grave is it?' Evie asked, trying not to show that she was a little disappointed by the state of the statue.

'Nobody my family was ever rich enough to hobnob with!' Grandma said, smiling. 'My lot are in the next row. Let's go and say hello to them.' She stepped high over some stinging nettles to reach the gravestone of her grandparents and of a child in the family who had died young. Next to it was the grave of Grandma's mother and father and her older brother, who had been killed in the Second World War.

Grandma was eighty-two years old now, but she never seemed that old to Evie. Grandma always said that she didn't mind being old – so long as she still felt fit enough to run for a bus if she wanted to. Evie's mother said that Grandma had better watch out that she didn't get run *over* by a bus, the way she was always dashing across the road to catch them.

'Shall we go and see Grandad's grave now?' Evie asked, wishing she'd brought some flowers to put on it. Her grandad had died before she was born, but she felt like she knew him because of everything Grandma had told her about him.

Grandad's grave was in the newer part of the graveyard, and when they got there they saw that there were daisy chains sitting on the top of all the headstones like crowns. The daisies looked bigger and brighter than ordinary ones. 'Who's put those there?' Evie asked in surprise.

'The fairies, I expect.' Grandma chuckled. 'They probably did it to cheer the place up a bit. I don't know what your grandad would say if *he* could see it, though – *he* never believed in them!'

'Lots of people don't believe in fairies, do they?' Evie said as she gazed in awe at all the decorated graves. 'Like Mum.'

Grandma sighed. 'It doesn't suit your mother to believe in fairies so she's convinced herself that she doesn't when really . . .' She broke off, frowning.

'I *do* believe in fairies,' Evie said quickly. 'But it's not as though I've ever actually *seen* one.'

'Just because you haven't seen one yet doesn't mean you *won't*,' Grandma said firmly. 'I didn't see *my* first fairy until I was forty years old.'

'*Forty?*' Evie gasped.

'That's right. I *believed* in them my whole life, mind. But I didn't see one until the day after I discovered I was going to have a baby.

Your grandad and I had tried for years to have children, but we'd never been blessed. And then I found out I was expecting, just as I had completely given up hope. I think I'd more or less given up hope of ever seeing a fairy too – but that day I remember thinking that anything was possible! And that's when I saw her. It was in this graveyard. She was called Buttercup. She had bright yellow hair and she was dressed in yellow – just like a buttercup herself! She made me a buttercup bracelet that lasted for months – right up until your mother was born.'

'Do you think there are fairies watching us now?' Evie started to look around in case one should suddenly appear.

'There might be. I wish I knew where to take you to see one, Evie, but I'm afraid I don't. Fairies don't like to be found, you see. They like to be the ones who find *you*.' She looked at Evie's disappointed face and seemed to make up her mind about something. 'There's one trick you can use to try to get them to visit you. Your mother made me promise not to tell you, but I don't see where the harm is . . .' She lowered her voice as if she thought a fairy might be eavesdropping. '*Chocolate!* All fairies love it! The ones round here seem to be especially partial to violet creams.'

'The kind Mum gives you every Christmas?' Evie asked, surprised. Every year Mum went to London just before

Christmas and bought Grandma a big box of violet and rose creams from a very expensive shop. Old ladies' chocolates, Evie's mother called them. She said they were too sweet and too perfumed for her liking but that Grandma had always loved them.

'That's right. I always save the violet ones for the fairies. I leave them on my window ledge at night and they're always gone in the morning.'

Evie dreaded to think what her mother would say if she could hear this. Those chocolates cost a fortune. Evie turned to look again at the daisy chain looped around her grandfather's gravestone. It seemed to be sparkling.

'It's the fairy dust they use that makes it sparkle like that,' Grandma said, following Evie's gaze. 'You'll have to ask them to decorate my grave like that when *I'm* buried here, Evie – if you've met any fairies by then!'

'Don't say that!' Evie said, frowning. *'You're* not going to die.'

'Of course I am. Everybody has to die sooner or later. Of course, I'd prefer it to be *later*, but I'd rather die while I'm still able to do everything for myself, than live to be a hundred, confined to my bed. Wouldn't you?'

Evie didn't reply. She understood what Grandma was saying – but she still wanted her to live to be a hundred if at all possible.

They made their way back to the house, where Evie's mother was busy packing. They were staying for tea first before heading home that evening.

Evie loved having tea at Grandma's because her grandmother baked lots of cakes whenever she knew they were

coming to stay. Evie's favourite was Grandma's ginger cake and her second favourite was the jam tarts. Grandma liked lemon-curd tarts the best, but Evie thought they were a bit too sweet. Today, because they were leaving, Grandma insisted on giving them the rest of the ginger cake to take home with them. She also produced a chocolate cake with butter-cream icing, which she had been keeping to send home with them as a present.

As soon as Mum went off to the kitchen to top up the teapot, Evie asked her grandmother, 'Do fairies like chocolate cake as well as chocolate? If I leave some of *that* on my window sill when I go to bed, do you think they'll come and get it?'

13

'The birds will come and get it!' Evie's mother said sharply. She had come back for the milk jug, which needed filling up too. 'Honestly, Evie, you're nine years old now. The other children will make fun of you if you talk like that when you go back to school.' She glared at Grandma as if she thought that it would be all her fault if Evie was teased.

Before Evie could protest that she was sure they wouldn't, Grandma intervened. 'I know you don't like it when I say this, my dear, but you always did worry far too much about what other people think.'

'And *you* never worried enough!' Evie's mother retorted. Evie was surprised by how emotional Mum sounded as she added, 'You certainly never worried what the other children thought about *me* when I was Evie's age!' She put the teapot down on the table, having clearly changed her mind about wanting another cup. 'Come on, Evie. We have to go now.'

'But we haven't finished tea yet!'

'You've had enough cakes. You'll be sick in the car if you eat any more.'

Evie looked at her grandmother for help, but Grandma was just staring in a frowning sort of way at Evie's mother as if she couldn't understand her at all.

Evie decided it was best not to ask for a piece of chocolate cake to put on her window ledge that night. By the time they got home she was very sleepy and Mum still seemed to be in quite a bad mood. It was great to see her dad again, though, and Evie managed to stay awake long enough to listen to the bedtime story he offered to read to her while Mum unpacked their things. Funnily enough, the story was about a fairy. Mum came in and listened to the end of it.

'Why don't you like fairies, Mum?' Evie murmured as her dad closed the book and kissed her goodnight.

'I do like fairies – in stories. That's where they belong.'

'But Grandma says—'

'I know what Grandma says and she's wrong.'

'But she says she's actually *seen* them!'

'The imagination can be a very powerful thing, Evie,' her mother said firmly, 'and your grandmother has always had a more active imagination than most people. You go to sleep now.' She kissed Evie and turned out her light.

Evie slept late the next morning and when she woke up she was surprised to hear her father's voice downstairs. Normally he would have gone to work by this time. She got up to see what was happening.

Her mother was sitting at the kitchen table, still in her dressing gown. Evie could tell that she'd been crying. Dad was

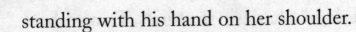

standing with his hand on her shoulder.

'What's wrong?' Evie asked.

Her mother looked up. 'Oh, Evie . . .'

It was Dad who told her. 'Grandma's cleaning lady phoned half an hour ago. She went round there at eight o'clock like she always does on a Tuesday and found your grandmother collapsed in her chair. She called an ambulance and then she called us. It seems like Grandma might have had a stroke. They've taken her into hospital.'

Evie knew what a stroke was. She had been with her mum to visit their next-door neighbour after she'd had a stroke last year. The old lady had nearly died and, even though she hadn't, she couldn't walk or talk properly afterwards. She'd had to sell her house and go and live in a nursing home where she could be looked after. Evie couldn't imagine Grandma being like that.

'But we only saw her yesterday,' Evie said. 'She was fine then.'

'These things can happen very suddenly, pet,' Dad told her.

'We don't know how serious it is yet,' Mum added. 'Though apparently she's unconscious . . .' Her eyes filled with tears again. '*Why* did I have to be so sharp with her yesterday?'

'I can take today off work and come to the hospital with you,' Dad offered. 'I have to go in to the office tomorrow – there's an important meeting – but at least I can drive you and Evie there today. I'll leave the car with you and come back on the train.'

'Thanks, darling.' Evie's mum wiped her eyes on a piece of kitchen towel. 'Evie and I can stay at Mum's house and visit her from there.' She looked at Evie. 'Thank goodness it's the school holidays.'

Not only did the school holidays mean that Evie didn't need to be at school, it also meant that her mum was off work too, since she worked as a school secretary.

Evie's dad made a couple of phone calls and went to change out of his work suit into some more comfortable clothes. Evie went to pack her suitcase again – which didn't take long since it was only half unpacked from the night before. She couldn't believe that only yesterday she had been chatting to Grandma about fairies. She glanced up at her old doll's house, which she had put out of the way on top of her wardrobe. Grandma had wanted her to take it with her the next time she visited. She decided to ask Dad if he would put it in the car for her.

Nobody talked much during the long drive. It was nearly afternoon when they arrived at the hospital and Evie had to stay in the waiting area while her parents went to see her grandmother and speak to the doctor. They were gone for such a long time that she got fidgety and decided to go and have a look in the hospital shop. They were selling chocolates there and among them was a small box of violet creams, which Evie had just enough money to buy.

When she got back to the waiting area her dad was there. 'You can come and see Grandma now,' he said, 'but you need to know she's very poorly.'

Something in his voice made Evie frightened. 'Is she like Mrs Evans?' Mrs Evans was the old lady who had lived next door.

Her father swallowed. 'We're not sure yet.' He looked at the box of chocolates in

Evie's hand. 'Sweetheart, she can't eat anything at the moment.'

'I know. I'm going to keep them at home for her. For when she gets better.' Because Grandma had to get better. She just had to.

Evie followed her dad down the corridor on to the ward where her grandmother was in a single room on her own. Evie's mum was sitting by her bed. Grandma was lying with her eyes closed, her soft grey hair looking much the same as normal. Evie could tell that she didn't have her teeth in and one side of her mouth seemed droopy. Apart from the drip, and another contraption with a syringe that she seemed to be attached to, she just looked like she was sleeping.

'Mum, Evie's here to see you,' her mother said, but Grandma didn't react. 'Here, darling,' Mum said to Evie, 'come and hold her hand.'

So that's what Evie did, only it didn't feel like she was holding Grandma's hand because her hand was so still.

When they got back to Grandma's house, Dad opened the boot of the car and Mum was surprised to see Evie's doll's house sitting next to their overnight bag. It was lucky the boot was so big, Evie thought, or it wouldn't have fitted in. Mum stared at it. 'Why have you brought that?'

'Grandma wanted me to,' Evie murmured.

Evie's Mum didn't say anything else but she exchanged a puzzled look with Evie's dad as he lifted the doll's house out of the boot and carried it into the house.

Dad had to set off for home again soon after that. When they'd dropped him off at the station, Mum busied herself with unpacking their things. Whenever they'd stayed with Grandma before, Mum had slept in the single bed in the spare room and Evie had slept there too, on the camp bed they brought with them from home. They hadn't remembered to bring the camp bed this time but Mum said it didn't matter. Now that Grandma was in hospital, Mum said she would sleep in her bed instead.

That night Evie found that she couldn't get to sleep even though she was really tired. In the end, she got up and went downstairs to the dining room, where Dad had put her doll's house. Grandma only ever used the dining room when she had visitors and the door was kept shut most of the time. The doll's house was still in the middle of the dining table and the moonlight was shining in on it. Mum had obviously forgotten to come in here before she went to bed because a window had been left open and the dining-room curtains hadn't been pulled.

Evie moved towards the doll's house. As she did, there was a noise of something being knocked over inside. A tiny voice said, 'Ouch!'

Evie froze.

Before she could investigate any further, the light came on in the hallway and her mum was calling out, 'Evie, is that you?' Seconds later, Mum was standing in the doorway, rubbing her eyes. 'What are you doing?'

Evie quickly turned her back on the doll's house and headed towards her mother. 'Nothing. I couldn't sleep.' She closed the dining-room door behind her before Mum could notice that anything was wrong.

'Neither can I. I know it's silly, but I'm really not liking being on my own tonight. Do you want to come and sleep in Grandma's bed with me? Maybe that would make us both feel better.'

Evie was only too pleased to agree.

She had never slept in Grandma's big brass bed before and as she climbed in she found that the mattress was very soft with springs that you could almost feel.

'I'm sure this is the same bed your grandma and grandad had when I was a child,' Mum said. 'It must be ancient.'

Evie snuggled up close to her mother, who reached out and turned off the bedside light. 'Do you think Grandma will wake up tomorrow?' she asked hopefully.

'Don't get your hopes up too much,' Mum warned her gently.

'I know, but . . .' Evie was remembering the conversation she'd had with Grandma only the day before – about how hoping for things was important. Hoping for something didn't always mean that you got it, Grandma had pointed out when they'd talked a bit more about it on their walk home, but if you gave up all your hopes and dreams, then you'd end up being a very sad person indeed.

'Do you think if I keep *hoping* to see a fairy, then one day I'll really see one?' Evie had asked her.

'To see a fairy you have to be in the right place at the right time in the right sort of mind,' Grandma had replied. 'Buttercup told me that. So the only thing you can do is make sure you're *always* in the right sort of mind – and then hope that one day you're in the right place when a fairy's about!'

As Evie drifted off to sleep she was thinking about the voice she had heard coming from her doll's house. Had she been imagining it? Or was it possible that her doll's house had already been occupied by its first fairy visitor? She decided that as soon as Mum was asleep she would sneak back downstairs to check. If only she wasn't starting to feel so sleepy herself . . .

Evie could feel something tickling her toes. She turned over to ask her mum if it was her, but found that her mum was fast asleep. The bedside clock with its illuminated hands showed that it was the middle of the night now. She must have fallen asleep too without realizing it. She could feel a funny breeze down by her toes, which was strange since she was lying under a sheet and blanket that were both tucked in at the bottom of the bed. She stuck her head under the covers to look down at her feet and to her amazement she saw two yellow lights.

Then she heard a voice. 'This is a very long tunnel.' The voice was light and tinkly like a fairy's.

As she shifted her position in the bed to see better, the lights suddenly went out.

Next to her, her mum was stirring. 'Evie, what is it?'

'Nothing,' Evie murmured, closing her eyes again. She must be dreaming, because fairies didn't live at the bottom of your bed. They lived at the bottom of your garden. Everyone knew that.

3

The next morning, Evie spotted that the little box of violet creams she had left on Grandma's dressing table had been opened. The cellophane had been ripped off and left beside the box, and when Evie looked inside there was one chocolate missing. Evie frowned. Her mum was the only person who could have eaten it, but her mum didn't like violet creams. Anyway, Mum wouldn't normally take anything of hers without asking.

Just then her mother came into the room looking for her hairbrush. She was yawning. 'I don't know about you but I had a terrible night's sleep in that bed. I hate soft mattresses.'

'I slept really well. I like this bed.' Evie touched the brass-bed frame fondly. Somehow, sleeping there made her feel closer to Grandma.

'Well, if you like it so much, do you want to sleep in it tonight and I'll take the other room?'

'OK,' Evie agreed enthusiastically. 'Mum,' she added, as her mother turned to go back into the bathroom, 'did you eat one of my violet creams?' Evie pointed at the little box on the dressing table. 'There's one missing.'

'Of course not. Didn't you eat it yourself?'

'No.'

Mum pulled a face as if she wasn't up for spending too much time thinking about violet creams right now. 'Maybe you ate it in your sleep.'

Evie went to inspect the box again. She remembered her dream from last night – at least she'd *thought* it had been a dream. *Could* those sparks of light at the bottom of her bed have been fairies after all? Grandma had told her that fairies liked to eat violet creams. Was it possible that instead of waiting for her to put one out on the window ledge they had come inside the house and helped themselves?

They visited Grandma again that afternoon and this time Mum left Evie alone with her while she went to speak to one of the doctors. While she was gone, Evie leaned closer to Grandma and whispered, 'I think I saw two fairies last night, Grandma. They were in your bed. I think they took one of your violet creams.'

Evie thought that Grandma's closed eyelids flickered slightly, but she couldn't be sure.

When she got home from the hospital she opened the box of violet creams and left it on the window ledge. Grandma had told her that fairies had a very good sense of smell, so if that was true maybe they would smell the chocolates and come back for more. She went to bed very early that evening, telling Mum she was tired, but really she just wanted to get to bed as quickly as possible in case the fairies came back.

Evie had left the curtains open and, as she lay on her side looking out of the window, she could see the moon. She waited and waited for a fairy to appear. Eventually, she heard her mum come up to bed and still there was no sign of any fairies. Her eyelids were starting to feel heavy so she let them close, thinking she would just rest them for a few seconds.

She opened them again when she heard tiny high-pitched voices. The room was brightly lit by moonlight now and when she glanced at Grandma's bedside clock she saw that it was three o'clock in the morning.

Evie's first thought was to rush to the window and look out, but she stopped herself. She didn't want to scare the fairies away. Then she realized that the voices weren't coming from the window. They seemed to be coming from inside the room, from the bottom of her bed. She felt movement under the sheet down by her feet, so she put her head underneath the covers to look. When she was younger she had sometimes snuggled right down under the covers, pretending she was in a real cave and that the bottom of her bed was really the start of a tunnel that led to all sorts of exciting places. She suddenly got that feeling again as the voices got louder, and she saw two sparks of light just like the night before.

Gradually, the sparks became bigger and brighter and Evie saw that they were coming from two fairy-sized lanterns. Then she saw the first fairy. The fairy was holding her lantern high above her head to keep the

covers off her as she flew up the bed. She was so small she could have sat on Evie's hand. The first thing that Evie noticed about her, apart from her beautiful shimmery wings, was the two white stars glowing in her hair. She was wearing a short pink floaty dress with pink stars embroidered on it. Her shiny dark hair was tied up in two bunches, each fastened with one of the stars. The second fairy was dressed in a floaty lilac dress, which was covered in little sparkles. Her hair was bobbed neatly at her shoulders and swung prettily when she moved her head, and she wore a dazzling crescent-moon hair clip.

The two fairies flew up the bed and out from between the sheets right in front of Evie's nose. She could see under their skirts as they flew across her face. They were both wearing sparkling fairy knickers that exactly matched their dresses. They didn't seem to realize she was watching them.

'Where are they?' the one with the stars in her hair whispered. 'Don't say she's eaten them already!'

'I know there's chocolate here somewhere. I can smell it!'

'Excuse me,' Evie said nervously, sitting up in bed. 'Can I help?'

Both fairies shrieked as if they'd just seen a ghost. The one with the moon hair clip nearly dropped her lantern.

'Please don't be frightened,' Evie added quickly. 'I *love* fairies. So does my grandma. She's seen lots, but you're the first ones I've ever met, so please don't fly away.'

The fairy with the pink dress recovered first. She flew back towards the bed, peering at Evie curiously. 'She *looks* harmless enough,' she said to her friend.

'I'm *very* harmless!' Evie said quickly. 'And if you stay and talk to me, you can have some more of my violet creams.'

'Are they yours then?'

'Sort of. I bought them for my grandma, but she isn't well enough to eat them.'

'She must be *very* sick if she can't eat violet creams!'

'She's had a stroke.' Evie's voice trembled slightly. 'She's in hospital.'

'Oh dear.' The fairy looked sorry.

Evie didn't really want to think about Grandma's illness right now so she said quickly, 'I can't believe you're really here! What are you called?'

'I'm Star,' the pink fairy replied, 'and this is Moonbeam.'

'What lovely names! Are you called Star because you've got stars in your hair – and Moonbeam because you've got a moon?'

'Oh, no – it's the other way round,' Star explained. 'I wear stars in my hair *because* I'm called Star. They're real ones, you know. I borrowed them from the Night Sky.'

'And I've got a moon in my hair because I'm called Moonbeam,' the other fairy said. 'The Night Sky couldn't lend me the real one, of course, but this is a very good copy, don't you think?' Before Evie could answer, she added, 'What's *your* name?'

'Evie.'

'We're very pleased to meet you, Evie,' the two fairies said in unison, giving little curtsies. Then they looked at each other and giggled.

'The fairy queen likes us to do that whenever we meet a human for the first time,' Moonbeam explained. 'She likes her fairies to have good manners.'

'Tell me about the fairy queen!' Evie

gasped, swinging her legs round to sit on the edge of the bed, still hardly believing this was really happening. 'Is she very beautiful?'

'Oh, yes. Fairy queens always are. Ours is called Queen Celeste and she rules over all us dream fairies.'

'*Dream* fairies! Is that what you are? Grandma's told me about fairies, but the ones she met were outside in the garden.'

'They would be flower fairies,' Star said. 'They're much more common than us. You won't find *us* in people's gardens. *We* live in Dreamland.' She said the last bit proudly.

'Dreamland?' Evie repeated, fascinated just by the sound of it. 'Where's that?'

'It's the most beautiful part of fairyland,' Star explained.

'That's what we think anyway,' Moonbeam put in. 'It's where dream fairies come from. It's very beautiful.'

'So are dream fairies *very* different from flower fairies?'

'Oh, yes,' Star replied. 'Our dresses are much sparklier and we wear matching knickers. Flower fairies don't, you know. *They* always wear knickers made out of plain white flower petals.' She pulled a face as if she found the thought of plain white knickers very boring indeed.

'Not so many humans know about us either,' Moonbeam added. 'That's because you have to fall asleep in a magic bed before we can visit you.'

'A *magic* bed?'

'That's right. This bed is magic. Otherwise we wouldn't be here!' Moonbeam flew over and landed on top of one of the brass bed knobs.

'But how can you tell it's magic?' Evie asked, staring at Grandma's bed. 'It doesn't *look* magic.' She wasn't sure exactly what a magic bed would look like, but Grandma's certainly wasn't sparkling with fairy dust or sprouting magic wings or doing anything else out of the ordinary.

'It's all to do with how a bed is made and who sleeps in it afterwards,' Moonbeam explained. 'First it has to be *made* by a person who believes in fairies.'

'And if lots of different people help to make the bed, they *all* have to believe in fairies,' Star added.

'And even after a magic bed has been made, it still has to get its magic switched on,' Moonbeam continued.

'*Switched on?*'

'That's right. For a magic bed to become *actively* magical – and able to transport dream fairies from Dreamland into your world – *three* humans who all believe in fairies have to sleep in the bed first. Not all at the same time, of course. One after another is fine. *Your* bed was activated last night when *you* slept in it – you must have been the third person to believe in fairies who did.'

'This is so . . . so cool!' Evie said. 'I just can't believe it's really happening!'

'Well, it is, and when you wake up tomorrow morning, you'd better not think we were just a dream,' Moonbeam warned her. 'A lot of humans do and it makes us very cross.'

'Of course, if you let us eat another chocolate then you'll have *proof* that we were really here,' Star pointed out. 'If you've got any left, that is.'

'Of course I've got some left! I put them on the window ledge for you.'

'The *window ledge*?' Star sounded horrified and immediately started to fly towards it.

'What's wrong?'

'Those greedy flower fairies are always stuffing their faces with things people leave out for them on window ledges,' she grumbled. 'Queen Celeste says it's no wonder they're getting so fat! We'll be lucky if—' She stopped abruptly and shrieked in delight as she saw the chocolate box still sitting there, lit up by the moonlight. 'Ooh, yummy!' She gasped as she descended on the chocolates and stuck her finger straight into the middle of a violet cream. She broke off a tiny bit of the chocolate coating and used it to scoop out a dollop of the fondant centre, which she stuffed into her mouth.

Evie watched as Moonbeam did the same – a little more delicately. 'It must be wonderful being a fairy,' she sighed. 'Though I expect you have to work really hard in fairyland, making magic potions and things to help people, don't you?'

'Oh, no,' Star mumbled through a mouthful of chocolate. 'Mostly what keeps us busy is all the parties we have to go to.'

'*Parties?*'

'That's right,' Moonbeam agreed, tearing a scrap of coloured tissue paper from the inside of the chocolate box and using it to dab the corners of her mouth. 'We have to make a different party dress for each party and it takes ages to sew on all the sequins.'

We *could* make our dresses sparkle with fairy dust if we wanted, but Queen Celeste says that would be a waste of good magic.'

As Moonbeam talked, Star was looking out over the garden warily, as if she expected a flower fairy to come and snatch the violet creams away from them at any minute. 'You know, I think it would be safer if we brought these chocolates inside and shut the window.'

'Don't worry, I won't let the flower fairies have any,' Evie said, smiling. She brought the violet creams back inside and the two fairies followed.

'We'd better be getting back now,' Moonbeam said. 'Queen Celeste doesn't like us keeping humans awake in the middle of the night for too long – she says it makes them grumpy.'

'Oh – please don't go yet!'

'We'll come back and visit you again soon,' Moonbeam promised.

Star was already lifting up the covers at the top of the bed to create the mouth of a cave for herself and Moonbeam to fly inside.

'Where do you go when you get to the bottom of the bed?' Evie asked them.

'Dreamland, of course!' And they both disappeared under the covers.

Evie climbed back into bed and looked down under the covers herself, snuggling right underneath like she used to. She worked her way down to the bottom of the bed where the fairies had come from – but there was nothing there.

4

Evie half expected Grandma to be sitting up in bed waiting for them when they got to the hospital the next day. She felt as if, now that she had actually seen a fairy, lots of other miraculous things might be about to happen.

But when they got to the ward, they found that the bed in Grandma's room was occupied by an elderly man. Evie immediately felt nervous without really knowing why.

'Don't worry,' Mum said quickly. 'Grandma must have been moved to another room or something. Wait here while I go and find out.' She went off to ask one of the nurses, leaving Evie standing where she was.

'They've moved her nearer to the nurses' station so they can keep an eye on her,' the old man in Grandma's room called out to her. 'She was a bit fidgety last night. Kept pulling out her drip. Not like me. I'm a good boy — I keep mine in.' He winked at her as he held up his arm with the drip attached.

Evie took a step inside the room. The man looked about the same age as Grandma, with wrinkled skin and hardly any hair. His blue eyes were smiling at her. 'My name's Harry,' he said. 'What's yours?'

'Evie . . .' She stared at him. 'You don't look very poorly.'

He chuckled. 'What? Think I'm wasting a good bed, do you?'

Evie flushed. 'I didn't mean that. It's just that my grandma can't sit up or talk or anything.'

He nodded, looking sympathetic. 'I guess

I'm not very poorly compared with her then, am I?'

Evie shook her head. 'What's wrong with you?' Because she knew people had to have *something* wrong with them to be in hospital.

'I had a nasty tummy bug. Couldn't keep anything down. Thought I'd be all right if I took to my bed for a few days but I got too weak to get up again. I live on my own so I didn't have anyone to help. Luckily, my fairy friends paid me a visit and found me like that. They went downstairs and found my walking stick and banged on the wall with it until my neighbour woke up. Then they unlocked the front door so she could get in. It was her who called the ambulance.'

'Your *fairy* friends?' Evie was getting interested now.

'That's right.' He winked at her. 'The

doctor says I must have been so sick that my mind was playing tricks on me, but I know differently.'

Just then Mum came back to tell her that Grandma had been moved to a different side room. Evie quickly said goodbye to Harry – she saw from the card above his bed that his name was Harold Watson – and followed her mother. Before they got to Grandma's new room, Mum stopped in the corridor and spoke very quietly to her. 'Evie, I've just had a talk with the nurse in charge of the ward. Grandma woke up last night.'

'*Woke up?*' Evie felt excited.

'Yes. She's been opening her left eye and moving her left arm. The right side of her body has been paralysed by the stroke so she can't move that. She isn't able to talk, though, and the nurses aren't sure how much she understands of what's said to her. She got very confused and agitated during the night but she's much calmer now.'

Evie asked anxiously, 'But will she get better?'

Mum swallowed. 'That's what I need you to understand. We don't know how much better she'll get. She might get a bit better than this – or she might not. You remember what Mrs Evans was like after her stroke, don't you?'

Evie frowned. She didn't *want* to remember what Mrs Evans was like.

Grandma was lying in bed looking much as she had the day before, except that her drip was attached to the opposite arm. She looked as if she was sleeping.

Evie went over and touched Grandma's arm, willing her to open her eyes and say something. Mum went round to the other side of the bed and stroked her forehead.

'Grandma . . . can you hear me?' Evie asked.

'She *might* be able to hear you,' Mum said gently. 'So talk to her as much as you want.'

Evie took a deep breath. 'I want to talk to her about the fairies.'

Mum didn't say anything for a few moments. Then, to Evie's surprise, she murmured, 'She loved to talk about the fairies, didn't she? If only I hadn't . . .' Mum's voice went hoarse and she suddenly let out a muffled sob and left the room.

Evie started to follow her, but saw that a nurse had gone to comfort her, so she went back and took Grandma's hand instead. She started to tell her about Star and Moonbeam. 'They're dream fairies, Grandma. Your bed is a magic bed, you see. That's how they can visit!'

Grandma suddenly opened her eyelids very slightly and looked at her.

'Grandma! It's me – Evie!'

Grandma seemed to be looking at her without seeing her. Then she closed her eyes and didn't respond when Evie tried to get her to open them again.

When Mum came back into the room Evie told her what had happened. 'She looked at me but I don't think she really knew who I was.'

Mum sat down beside Grandma's bed and looked at her mother. 'Why don't you go to the hospital shop and choose some flowers for her, Evie? Then, if she opens her eyes again, there'll be something bright and cheerful for her to see.'

'Grandma likes yellow flowers the best,' Evie said, as Mum handed her some money.

'You're right,' Mum agreed. 'She used to love taking me primrose picking in the spring when I was little. And I remember your grandad used to buy her yellow roses.'

'I'll see if they have any yellow flowers in the shop.'

Evie had to pass Harry's room to get there, and Harry waved to her as she went by. She waved back, remembering what he had told her about *his* fairy friends. She wondered if they had been dream fairies too, and decided that when she got the chance, she would go and ask him.

Evie had to wait until the following night for Moonbeam and Star to come back again. She was in need of cheering up because Dad had phoned that evening to say that he wasn't going to be able to make it to Grandma's that weekend as he had to work.

'Evie! Open your eyes! We've got a surprise for you!'

She woke to find that her room was sparkling with fairy lights. Star and Moonbeam had draped them all around the walls, and across the window, and all along the top of Grandma's dressing table. The two fairy lanterns were sitting in the middle of the floor and, in between them, the fairies had unfolded one of Grandma's yellow cotton hankerchiefs and placed some tiny plates of sparkly food on top.

'You gave us those lovely violet creams,' Star said, 'so we thought we'd bring some fairy food for *you* to taste.'

Evie felt very excited as she sat cross-legged on the floor in front of the fairy picnic. Star and Moonbeam began lifting up the tiny star-shaped plates to offer her things, clearly excited too.

The first thing they gave her was a sparkling biscuit, which fizzled in her mouth and tasted of strawberries. 'That's a magic fruit biscuit,' Moonbeam told her. 'It tastes of your favourite fruit.'

'Now try one of these,' Star said, offering her a different plate. 'These ones taste like your *second*-favourite fruit.'

The second biscuit tasted of bananas. 'I've never been able to decide whether I like strawberries or bananas best!' Evie gasped.

'Well, now you know. Here –' Star offered her a plate of what looked like pink raindrops – 'these are cloud-burst sweeties. You suck them and they stop you being thirsty.'

'Try a cloud tart as well,' Moonbeam said, handing her a tiny pastry with a fluffy white centre.

As Evie ate it and pronounced it delicious, Star asked, 'Queen Celeste really likes violet creams, so we were wondering if we could take one back to fairyland for her? There's no such thing as chocolate in fairyland, you see.'

'No such thing as chocolate?' Evie was surprised. She had always imagined that fairyland was a place where you could have anything you wanted. She pointed to the chocolate box, which was still on the dressing table. 'Help yourselves.'

'Thanks.' Star flew over to the box straight away.

Then Evie thought of something. 'Wait, I've got a better idea! Why don't you bring her here to eat it? I'd really love to meet her.'

'Queen Celeste never travels out of fairyland,' Moonbeam explained. 'She travelled a lot when she was younger, but now she feels that her place is at home so she can be there if any of her fairies need her.'

'Oh.' Evie did her best to hide her disappointment as she watched Star trying to lift out a whole violet cream from the box without getting sticky fingermarks on it. She told herself that it didn't really matter, though, since there were other things that were more important than getting to meet the fairy queen.

'There's something I wondered if *you* could do for *me*,' she began timidly.

'What?' Both fairies turned to look at her.

'Well . . . you can do magic, can't you?'

'Of course.'

'So . . . so can you make people better if they're sick?'

59

'It depends *how* sick.'

'It's my grandma, you see . . .' Evie explained. 'She's *very* sick. She might be too sick *ever* to get better. And I really want her to get better and come home again so she can meet you. She believes in fairies too, you see, so I know she'd love to meet you . . .' Evie trailed off.

Moonbeam and Star were frowning.

'Fairies aren't able to do anything when humans are *very* sick,' Moonbeam told her gently. 'Fairies can't interfere in human matters of life and death, you see.'

'But there must be *something* you can do?' Evie felt her voice starting to tremble. '*Please?*'

Moonbeam and Star looked at each other. 'You say she believes in fairies?'

'She's believed in them all her life!'

'There is *something* we might be able to

do . . .' Moonbeam said cautiously, still looking at Star. 'Don't you think?'

Star nodded. She was looking thoughtful. 'We might be able to take her on a trip to fairyland.'

'Could you really do that?'

'We *might* be able to. But we don't normally take adults to fairyland so you'd have to ask Queen Celeste first. She sometimes meets children in a special meeting room in her fairy palace. There's a magic way we could take you there – if you don't mind being shrunk down to the size of a fairy.'

'But that's only if Queen Celeste *agrees* to have a meeting with you,' Moonbeam added quickly. 'You'd have to write to her first, explaining why you want to see her.'

'I'll write her a letter now!' Evie said, getting excited. 'Then you can take it with you!'

'Oh, no, we can't do that! You'll have to find a fairy postbox and post it yourself. Queen Celeste says that any human child who can't find a fairy postbox can't have enough fairy sense to be worth allowing into fairyland.'

'*Fairy* sense?' Evie was puzzled.

'Yes. You've heard of *common* sense, haven't you?'

Evie nodded.

'Well, *fairy* sense is the opposite of that. Most humans have too much common sense and not enough fairy sense, and Queen Celeste says it's not worth showing *them* round fairyland because afterwards they'll just think they've dreamt the whole thing. And that makes it a big waste of time from our point of view.'

'*I* wouldn't think I'd dreamt it!'

'Which is why you're sure to find a fairy postbox straight away. Children with lots of fairy sense always do.'

'But I don't know what a fairy postbox looks like,' Evie said, watching Star fly across the room with a violet cream balanced on her head.

'Oh, that doesn't matter. You'll probably find one more easily if you *don't* know what you're looking for.'

'But that doesn't make sense!' Evie protested.

'It makes *fairy* sense,' Star and Moonbeam replied firmly. Then, with a flourish of fairy dust, Moonbeam had cleared away the remains of the picnic and all the fairy lights, and both fairies had vanished under the covers of Grandma's bed.

Evie got up the next morning and wrote her letter to the queen of the dream fairies.

Dear Queen Celeste, she wrote, *I am writing to ask if you would please let me come and see you at your palace in fairyland. I really need to speak to you about my grandma. Love from, Evie*

She read it back to herself and added, *P.S. I don't mind being shrunk.*

Then she put the letter in an envelope and wrote, *Queen Celeste, Queen of the Dream Fairies, Fairyland*, on the front.

Now all she had to do was find a fairy postbox.

She started by searching out in the

garden. It had been raining during the night so the grass was wet. She didn't really expect to see a fairy postbox sitting in the middle of Grandma's lawn so she went to the bottom of the garden instead. Maybe she would find a tree with a hole cut in the trunk and a fairy would come along while she was standing there and post a letter in it. Then she would know it was a fairy postbox.

There were two trees at the bottom of Grandma's garden, but when Evie inspected them neither had any holes in their trunks. She went to look in the flower beds instead. She was sure that a fairy postbox wouldn't look like an ordinary postbox. Maybe what she was looking for was a special bush with fairy dust sprinkled on it or something. But all the bushes and flowers in Grandma's garden were covered in raindrops, not fairy dust, though she did find the perfect spot

behind a bush where she could set up her doll's house for the flower fairies.

Evie kept searching but she couldn't find anything that looked like it might be a postbox, and in the end she went back inside the house. Maybe a fairy postbox was really tiny, like a fairy, and therefore difficult

to see. But the letter she had written wasn't fairy-sized. It was human-sized, written on Grandma's best notepaper. So any postbox she posted it in was going to have to be quite big too.

By the time Evie went with her mum to visit Grandma that afternoon, she was feeling fed up. Moonbeam had made it sound like it would be easy to find a fairy postbox, but it seemed like she was wrong. And if Evie couldn't post her letter to Queen Celeste, how was she going to help Grandma? As Evie followed Mum on to the ward she noticed that the old man she had met – Harold Watson – was sitting up in bed reading. She wondered if he was going to have any visitors today. She hoped he would, because it must be lonely to be in hospital and *not* have any visitors.

Grandma was asleep again when they

went into her room. Evie sat looking at her for a while. Having Grandma so close, and yet so far away from her at the same time, was horrible and Evie suddenly felt like she couldn't stand it any longer.

'Where are you going?' Mum asked as she stood up and made for the door.

'For a walk,' Evie replied.

Mum nodded like she understood. 'All right, but don't go far.'

Evie went as far as Harry's room and stopped. 'Hello, Mr Watson.' She hovered awkwardly in the doorway.

He looked up from his book and smiled at her. 'Hello, there. It's Evie, isn't it? How are you today?'

'All right. Can I come in?'

'Of course. How's your grandma?'

'Not very well.'

He closed his book. 'I'm sorry to hear that.

I expect that's why you're looking a bit gloomy, is it?'

Evie nodded. 'But it's not just that. It's—' She broke off, wondering whether to tell him the rest. He might be able to help her. After all, he knew about fairies, so maybe he knew about fairy postboxes too. 'You know how you told me you saw fairies when you were in your bed at home . . . ?' she began cautiously. 'Well, I was wondering . . . were they *dream* fairies?'

Harry looked surprised. 'I see you know a lot about fairies. They *are* dream fairies, as a matter of fact. They've been visiting me on and off for years now. How did you guess?'

'Some dream fairies came to visit me too when I fell asleep in Grandma's bed.'

'Really?' He looked extremely interested now. 'An *old* bed, is it?'

She nodded.

'Brass?'

She nodded again. 'The thing is, I want to post a letter to their fairy queen but I can't find a fairy postbox. I'm supposed to have enough fairy sense to find one, but I don't think I have.'

Harry looked thoughtful. 'You look like you've got plenty of fairy sense to me. Where have you looked so far for this fairy postbox?'

'Well, I searched the whole of Grandma's garden this morning.'

'Hmm . . . It seems to me that the garden is the sort of place where a *flower* fairy might put a postbox. *Dream* fairies are a different kettle of fish altogether.'

'How do you mean?'

'Well, think about it. Where would you go to find a dream fairy?'

'I don't know. I'd have to wait for one to

visit me while I was asleep, I suppose.'

'Exactly. So if you want to find a dream fairy's postbox, shouldn't you look for that when you're asleep too?'

Evie frowned. 'But that's silly. I mean, nobody can look for something when they're asleep.'

'Can't they? Not even if they've got fairy sense?' Suddenly Harry looked past her and smiled. A grey-haired lady who looked quite a bit older than Mum was standing in the doorway. 'Margaret, you made it! Evie, I'd like you to meet my daughter. Evie and I were just having a chat about fairy matters, Margaret.'

'Fairy matters, eh?' Harry's daughter rolled her eyes in a way that made it clear that she didn't believe in fairies any more than Mum did. She came over and put a bunch of grapes on the locker beside Harry's bed. 'Don't believe everything he tells you,' she said lightly to Evie. 'Sorry I'm late, Dad, but the traffic was really bad. It took four hours to get here. I wish you lived a bit closer. It's nice to find you've already got a visitor, though.'

'I'm really meant to be visiting my grandma,' Evie said quickly. 'I'd better go back now.' She said goodbye and left Harry with his daughter.

She thought over what he had said. If he was right, she would need to wait until she went to bed tonight to find a fairy postbox. But she still couldn't see how anyone could find a postbox while they were sleeping . . .

It took Evie a long time to fall asleep that night because she was worrying so much about what would happen when she did.

Harry had seemed so sure that she would somehow be able to post her letter in her sleep, but she still couldn't imagine how.

She went to bed with the letter in her hand anyway, and as she closed her eyes and began to drop off she found herself imagining what a fairy postbox might look like in the place where dream fairies lived. Perhaps all the postboxes would be floating on clouds. Or perhaps they would be decorated with stars from the Night Sky, like the ones in Star's hair . . .

Evie was soon dreaming about being in fairyland. In her dream she had a letter in her hand and was stepping on to a shimmery white pathway. She carefully moved her feet along the moonbeam path until she saw a postbox in the distance that was the same size and shape as the one on the corner of her road at home. It wasn't the same colour, though. Instead of being red, it was a brilliant white, decorated all over with sparkling stars, and it was sitting on what looked like a puff of cloud. She saw that a little footbridge led from the end of the moonbeam path on to the cloud and, as she crossed the bridge, the rectangular mouth of the postbox changed into a big, red-lipped, smiling mouth that actually spoke to her. 'Is that letter for me?'

Evie jumped. 'Y-yes,' she stammered. 'Well, it's for Queen Celeste really.'

'There's no stamp on the envelope,' the postbox pointed out.

'Oh ...' Evie stared helplessly at the letter in her hand. It hadn't occurred to her that she might need something as ordinary as a stamp to post a letter to the fairy queen.

'All letters to dream fairies have to be stamped with a star or I can't accept them. But don't worry. You can use one of *my* stars. Make sure it's stuck down firmly, though. I don't want it falling off inside my belly. Stars can be very tickly when they get stuck inside your belly.'

Evie looked nervously at the stars that were decorating the postbox. They were so beautiful that she somehow didn't like to touch them.

'Don't worry,' the postbox reassured her. 'They're quite used to being borrowed to put on letters.'

Evie carefully peeled off a small shiny star and placed it in the top right-hand corner of her envelope. She gave the letter a shake to make sure the star was firmly in place. 'Shall I put it inside your mouth then?' she asked the postbox shyly.

'That's right. Then I'll take it to Queen Celeste.'

As Evie crossed the bridge back on to the moonbeam path she saw the postbox start to float away on its cloud.

She was starting to feel very sleepy. The path she was walking on seemed to be going on forever. Maybe if she just lay down where she was for a few minutes and rested . . .

When Evie woke up the next morning, she immediately remembered her dream about the talking postbox. If only you really *could* post a letter in your dreams, she thought.

She got up and it was only after she had washed and got dressed that she thought of her letter to Queen Celeste. She went back and looked for it inside the bed, under the bed, down the side of the bed and everywhere else in Grandma's bedroom that she could think of, but she couldn't find it anywhere.

She sat down at Grandma's dressing table, frowning. Could it be that she really *had* posted Queen Celeste's letter in her dream last night after all? Her common sense told her that was impossible. But what was her *fairy* sense telling her?

6

Evie spent the whole of that day wondering if Queen Celeste had received her letter. She visited Grandma as usual in the afternoon and she tried to visit Harry too, but he wasn't in his room. The nurse told her he was having a bath.

She went to bed early and, in the middle of the night, she was woken by familiar fairy voices. She opened her eyes to see Star and Moonbeam sitting on her pillow.

'If you sprinkle fairy dust on her top half, I'll do the bottom,' Moonbeam was saying. 'That should work, shouldn't it?'

'So long as we don't leave a gap in between.'

Evie sat up quickly. 'What are you talking about?'

'Oh, you're awake! We're just talking about how we're going to shrink you.'

'Has Queen Celeste said I can come then?' Evie asked, excitedly.

'Yes. She got your letter and she says you obviously have plenty of fairy sense as well as very neat handwriting. So you can come with us to Dreamland. We can take you now if you want.'

'*Now?*'

'Yes . . . well . . . after we've had one of your chocolates. Shrinking spells can be quite hard work. We'll need something to keep our strength up.'

Evie felt her heart beating faster as she got up to fetch the chocolates for them. 'What happens? Do I just lie in bed and let you shrink me, or what?'

'Yes, but you'd better get dressed first. You don't want to find yourself in Queen Celeste's palace in your pyjamas, do you?'

Evie put on the only smart summer dress she had brought with her to Grandma's, while Star and Moonbeam shared a violet cream. 'I've got a sparkly necklace too. Shall I wear that?' she asked as she sat down at the dressing table to brush her hair.

'Oh, yes! Queen Celeste loves sparkly things!'

'Will it hurt, getting shrunk?' Evie asked, feeling a bit nervous as she got back under the covers.

'Oh, no. Not if we do it right.' Star started to sprinkle something that looked like gold-coloured dust over Evie's head as Moonbeam flew down under the covers to sprinkle more dust over her bottom half.

'What if you *don't* do it right?' Evie asked

anxiously. But she didn't get an answer — which was probably just as well. She was starting to feel very strange indeed.

'Close your eyes,' Star ordered, 'and don't open them until we tell you.'

Evie did as she was told. She felt her skin tingling all over and the sheets slowly

moving over her in a way that was quite ticklish.

'OK, you can open your eyes now!' Star called out.

Evie found that she was lying on the floor of a vast white tent. She stood up and discovered that the ground was soft and springy. The tent was lit only by the two lanterns Star and Moonbeam were holding above their heads. Her two fairy friends were the same size as her now – as if they had changed from fairies into little girls with wings. Then Evie remembered that it wasn't Star and Moonbeam who had changed size – it was her. The springy ground she was standing on was really Grandma's mattress, and the sides of the tent were the sheets.

'You'd make a very pretty fairy,' Star said, peering at her in the lantern light, 'though

you look a bit funny without any wings.'

'Follow us!' Moonbeam ordered, starting to fly down what looked like a long dark tunnel but was actually still the inside of Evie's bed.

The fairies' shimmery wings created a strong breeze as they flew. Evie tried to keep up with them but found that she kept losing her balance as she struggled to walk on the springy ground.

'It's much easier if you fly,' Star said, stopping to wait for her. 'You can fly with us if you like.' The fairies each took one of Evie's hands and they lifted her up into the air.

Now that Evie was able to fly through the tunnel with them, the fairies seemed to be going faster and faster.

'Shouldn't we have got to the bottom of the bed by now?' Evie asked.

'Magic beds don't have bottoms,' Star explained. 'Well, not on the inside anyway. They lead all the way to Dreamland.'

'We're going to switch to top speed now,' Moonbeam told her. 'Otherwise it'll take all night to get there.'

For the rest of the journey Evie felt like she was hurtling through a black hole at lightning speed and she wondered if this was how it felt to be an astronaut speeding away from Earth in a rocket.

Suddenly the tunnel came to an end and they shot out into a huge open space.

'Where are we?' Evie gasped, as she took in the black sky lit up by stars, and the moon, huge and white, above them.

'In Dreamland,' Star replied. 'This is where we live.'

Evie stared around her in awe. There was nothing under her feet, so it was just as well that Star and Moonbeam were holding on to her. Floating in the sky around them were lots of clouds in the shape of houses, with doors and windows and little floating gardens attached. The cloud houses were clearly moving about, but miraculously they weren't bumping into each other. There didn't seem to be any continuous ground here at all. A big grassy area with flowers and trees was floating in the middle of the houses, and Moonbeam told her that that was the park.

'We have a massive party there whenever there's a Blue Moon,' Moonbeam said. 'We all have to wear blue and the Moon is our guest of honour. It's great fun! We even have blue fireworks!'

'What's a Blue Moon?' Evie asked.

'Oh, it's just what happens when the Moon is feeling sad. If you looked up at him you'd see he was blue instead of his normal colour. It never lasts long because we're always here to throw him a party to cheer him up.'

'Look! That's the dream garden over there,' Star said, pointing to another garden, which was surrounded by a wall covered in glowing white flowers. It had a little house attached to it and pink smoke was coming from the chimney.

'Who lives *there*?' Evie asked.

'That's the dreamkeeper's cottage,' Star explained. 'We all take it in turns to stay there and look after the garden. It's quite a difficult job because the garden changes all the time depending on what dreams are going on inside.'

'How do you mean?'

'Queen Celeste will explain everything. We have to follow the star path through the Night Sky to get to her palace. There's the path over there. Come on.' Moonbeam folded in her wings to land on the shiny path, which seemed to be made from large stars lying flat like paving stones. Evie watched Moonbeam tread lightly on each star as she followed behind her. Star was following Evie, skipping along and humming a tune. The path seemed to be leading them up through the Night Sky, twisting its way in between cloud houses and other bits of the fairy town – if you could call it that – until they came to a huge white cloud that completely blocked their path.

'Queen Celeste's palace is through here,' Moonbeam said, stepping inside the cloud and disappearing.

'Go on,' said Star, giving Evie a little shove from behind.

Evie stepped into the cloud too – and gasped as she emerged out the other side. Ahead of her was a beautiful palace. Its walls were pearl coloured and it had four round turrets and numerous brightly lit,

star-shaped windows. The massive silver front door was set in an archway of twinkling stars, and the whole building seemed to be shimmering in the moonlight. It was sitting on a big pink cloud, around the edge of which was a pink hedge that seemed to be completely covered in the same brilliant white flowers that Evie had seen decorating the walls of the dream garden.

'Let's put a moonflower in your hair!' Star suggested. She went and picked a white flower from the hedge and gave it to Evie.

'It's beautiful,' Evie said, turning it round in her hand. The flower seemed to be glowing just like the moon.

'I know. The flower fairies keep begging us for cuttings, but there's no point in *them* trying to grow them. Moonflowers will only grow in Dreamland.'

'Hurry up,' Moonbeam called to them impatiently. She was already banging the big star-shaped knocker on the front door of the palace. The silver door swung open just as Star and Evie caught up with her.

Evie stepped nervously inside to find herself in a large hallway, with walls that were also glowing. She looked up and couldn't see a roof. All that was visible was the Night Sky, filled with twinkling stars.

A pretty fairy in a yellow dress was sitting on a stool in the corner playing a golden harp. As Evie listened to the music she started to feel more relaxed.

'Queen Celeste likes to have fairy music playing in her palace all the time,' Star explained. 'You're lucky this isn't a fairy lullaby. You'd fall asleep straight away if it was. Fairy lullabies work especially fast on humans.'

Several fairies in different pastel-coloured dresses were appearing now from various doorways off the hall. Moonbeam quickly explained who Evie was and that she had come to see the fairy queen.

'You'd better show her into the Meeting Room then,' said a fairy in a turquoise dress. 'I'll go and tell Queen Celeste she's here.'

Moonbeam led Evie across the hall and into a very grand-looking room. There was a huge ornamental fireplace at one end with a vase of moonflowers sitting in the hearth. A long table that seemed to be made entirely from a beam of light stretched across the length of the room. It felt as solid as a beam of wood when Evie touched it, though, and so did the matching benches on either side of the table.

'Wait here. Queen Celeste won't be long,' Moonbeam said.

As soon as she was alone in the room, and Moonbeam had closed the door so she could no longer hear the harp music, Evie started to feel nervous again. What if Queen Celeste wasn't as easy to talk to as Star and Moonbeam? And what if she got cross when she heard why Evie had come?

Suddenly a door at the back of the room opened and a tall, elegant fairy in a long floaty dress entered. She had silky dark hair that fell to her waist and cornflower-blue eyes. Her lips were shimmery pink. She was wearing a crown of real stars, and her dress seemed to change colour as she walked. First it was a plain light blue and then the blue was covered in white clouds. Then the dress became a much darker blue and the clouds became grey with sun rays shining out from behind them. Finally the dress changed to a blue-black colour and started to sparkle with tiny stars.

Evie was so busy staring at the fairy queen's dress that she completely forgot to curtsy. Queen Celeste didn't seem to mind, though.

'You must be Evie,' she said, smiling.

Evie nodded, still unable to take her eyes from the dress.

'My gown is made from a length of real sky. That's why it's so changeable. Do you like it?'

'Oh, yes!' Evie looked up at Queen Celeste's face. 'Th-thank you for letting me come,' she stammered shyly.

'Are you enjoying your visit?'

'It's . . . it's wonderful!'

'Good. Now . . .' She sat down and gestured for Evie to do the same. 'What was it that you wanted to ask me?'

Evie swallowed. Now that she had the fairy queen right in front of her she was almost too afraid to ask. 'I know . . . I know Star and Moonbeam said you don't normally let grown-ups come to fairyland . . .' she began hesitantly, 'but I'd really like it if my grandma could come. She believes in fairies and I'm sure she's got lots of fairy sense. She's very sick, you see. She's in hospital and we don't think . . . we don't *know* . . . if she'll ever be well enough to come home again.'

'Star and Moonbeam have already told

me a little about your grandmother,' Queen Celeste replied. 'You do understand that we won't be able to make her better, even if she comes here, don't you?'

Evie nodded.

'We can't use our shrinking spell on her because her body isn't well enough for that. But we could bring her here in her dreams instead – we do that sometimes for children whose bodies are very sick.'

'In her *dreams*?' Evie didn't understand.

'You see, your grandma's body isn't much use to her any more so she might as well leave it behind. That way we can bring her to our magic dream garden while she sleeps – and her poor old body can just stay where it is in bed.'

Evie didn't really understand how that could happen, but she didn't like to question Queen Celeste any further. 'Star and

Moonbeam showed me the dream garden on the way here and I was wondering what was inside.'

'That depends on the dreamer,' Queen Celeste told her. 'The dreamer can choose anything or anyone they want to be inside.'

'Any*one*?'

Queen Celeste nodded. 'But any *person* who enters the dream garden has to believe in fairies *and* be sleeping in a magic bed.' She paused. 'Which brings us to our problem.'

'What?'

'Your grandmother has to be sleeping in a magic bed herself before we can bring her here – and her hospital bed isn't magical.'

'But she isn't well enough to leave hospital!'

'I know. But it might be possible to transfer the magic from her old bed to her hospital bed.'

'Can you do that?'

'*I* can't. But *you* might be able to.'

'*Me?*'

'Yes.' Queen Celeste reached into a pocket in her dress and pulled out a shiny white envelope, which she handed to Evie.

'This will explain how. Read it when you get home.'

Suddenly the door to the hallway opened and harp music could be heard again, only this time the tune was different. Evie started to feel incredibly sleepy.

'The fairy lullaby will take you home now,' Queen Celeste told her. And before Evie could reply, she had fallen asleep.

7

Evie woke up the next morning in Grandma's bed to find that she was holding a tiny white envelope in her hand. Nothing was written on the outside, but Evie knew it was the one the fairy queen had given her. The letter had seemed a normal size last night, but now that Evie was back to *her* normal size it was so tiny she wasn't sure she'd be able to read it.

Evie carefully opened the envelope and found a folded piece of very delicate paper inside. It was folded over so many times that when she opened it up completely it was the same size as a human letter.

Except that there was nothing written on it.

Evie turned it over but the paper was blank on both sides. Evie couldn't understand it. Queen Celeste had told her that the instructions she needed to make Grandma's hospital bed magical would be in the letter.

Evie felt frustrated for the rest of that morning and when she went to the hospital with Mum in the afternoon she decided to take the fairy letter with her to show Harry.

She sat with Grandma for a while, listening to Mum telling her how lovely her garden was looking. Grandma's eyes flickered once or twice but apart from that she didn't respond. 'I'm just going to see Mr Watson,' Evie said, slipping out of the room while Mum was rearranging Grandma's flowers.

Harry was sitting in his chair in his dressing gown and he didn't have his drip attached any more. He was sipping a cup of tea and eating a biscuit.

'Are you better?' Evie asked him.

'*Much* better. The doctor says I can go home in a day or two.'

Evie frowned. She had got used to Harry being here. Still, it was good that he was well enough to leave the hospital.

'I'll miss your visits, though,' Harry added, as if he could sense what she was thinking.

'Will anyone visit you when you go home?'

'My daughter – when she can. And I've got a few friends in the village. Then there are my fairy friends, of course. I should think they'll be along to see me pretty soon.'

'You should leave some chocolate out for them,' Evie said. 'Then they'll *definitely* come.'

Harry smiled. 'Don't I know it! Greedy little things, aren't they?

'Star is the greediest. She gets chocolate all round her face. Moonbeam isn't so bad.'

'Star and Moonbeam, eh? Mine are called Sky and Twinkle.'

'Mr Watson, can I show you something?' Evie was pulling the fairy envelope out of her pocket. She didn't tell him the whole story about her visit to Dreamland, but she did explain about the fairies giving her a letter. 'But when I opened it there was nothing written on it,' she finished, showing it to him.

Harry took the letter from her and turned it over in his hand. 'I got a birthday card from my fairies once,' he said.

'Did you?'

'It was my eightieth birthday and they left me a star-shaped card. It didn't look like anything special at first and there was no writing on it to say who it was from. But when night-time came and the moonlight was shining in through my window, the card started to twinkle just like a real star. And on the back there was fairy writing. It said, HAVE A MAGIC BIRTHDAY, HARRY!' He chuckled as he remembered. 'I've still got it but the fairy dust has worn off now so you can't read the message even in the moonlight.'

'Do you think there'll be writing on my letter if I read it in the moonlight, then?' Evie asked, suddenly feeling more hopeful.

'I wouldn't be surprised.' Harry watched as Evie carefully folded up her letter and returned it to its tiny envelope. 'Tell me something, Evie . . . Has your grandmother lived round here for a long time?'

Evie nodded. 'All her life. Why?'

'Well, ever since you told me about your grandma's brass bed, I've been wondering . . . Before I retired I used to make brass beds, you see. I had a little workshop in a village near here. And what with hers being a magic bed, I've been wondering if it could be one of mine . . . Do you know when she bought it?'

'Before my mum was born, I think,' Evie said.

'I wonder if they bought it from my shop. There can't be that many shops around here that were making magic beds.' He looked at her. 'Did the fairies tell you how a magic bed is made?'

Evie nodded. 'The person who makes it has to believe in fairies, and then three people who believe in fairies have to sleep in it.'

'I only found that out myself when my niece came to see me with her children one day. It was more than ten years ago now. The children were tired so they went upstairs to have a nap on my bed. It was that night that

I first saw the fairies. The children must have activated the magic – and I was the one who had made the bed. My daughter didn't believe me when I told *her* about it, of course. She'd moved away long before that. Married with two boys of her own, she was, by that time.' Harry asked Evie to pass him his wallet from the bedside cabinet so that he could show her a photograph of his two grandsons. 'Both of them are college students now. Nice lads, but I don't see them as often as I'd like.'

'I don't think my grandma saw me . . . I mean, sees me . . . as often as she'd like either,' Evie said. Suddenly she felt guilty about leaving Grandma to come and chat to Harry. 'I'd better go back now.'

'Let me know how you get on with reading that letter, won't you?' Harry said, and she promised that she would.

*

As soon as the moon came out that evening, Evie took the fairy letter out into the back garden and opened it up. Since her conversation with Harry, she had found herself wondering why Queen Celeste hadn't told her how to read the letter when she'd given it to her. Unless she was testing her fairy sense again. Evie felt a little guilty when she thought how it was really *Harry's* fairy sense that had told her what to do – especially as he had told her where to look for the fairy postbox too.

But Evie didn't have time to worry about that because as the moonlight shone down on the letter something strange began to happen. The paper began to sparkle, just as if it was covered in fairy dust. Then gold writing appeared on it. Evie held her breath as she started to read what Queen Celeste had written.

*

A magic bed can transfer its magic to an ordinary bed in the following way:

The person or persons who made the magic bed AND the three people who activated the bed's magic must all be found. They must link hands around the new bed. When the chain of people is complete, the new bed will sparkle with fairy dust while the magic reaction takes place, and from then on it will be a magic bed. But be warned – doing this will completely drain the magic from the original bed.

Evie got a bit of a shock when she read the last sentence. If Grandma's old bed lost its magic, then Evie wouldn't be able to see Star and Moonbeam again. But if this was the only way Grandma could get to fairyland, she knew she had no choice.

Evie studied the letter for a long time. She would somehow have to get all the people mentioned by Queen Celeste to stand around Grandma's hospital bed together – if she could find them. Harry thought he had made Grandma's brass bed – but she would have to find out for sure. And Grandma and herself were two of the people who had activated the bed – but who was the third?

'Mum, did any other children ever come and stay here with Grandma?' Evie asked after she had gone back inside the house. She guessed that the third person had probably been a child rather than a grown-up, since children tended to believe in fairies more than adults did.

Mum was in the kitchen making cocoa. She didn't usually drink cocoa, but she said that staying in the house where she'd spent her childhood was reminding her of all the things she had loved when she was younger. And cocoa was one of them. 'Why?'

'No reason. I was just wondering.'

'One of my cousins came over from Canada once, with her children, but I think they stayed in a hotel.'

'Could any of them have gone upstairs for a nap on Grandma's bed while they were here, do you think?' Evie asked, remembering Harry's story about how *his* magic bed had been activated.

'Why do you want to know that?'

'It's just . . . just . . .' Suddenly she had an idea. 'It's just a survey I'm helping Mr Watson with. He thinks Grandma's brass bed is one of the ones *he* made, you see, and

he wants to know how many different people have slept in it.'

Mum almost laughed. 'Why on earth does he want to know *that*?'

'I told you. Because he's doing a *survey*.' Evie knew that people did surveys to find out all sorts of daft things. Her mum had got one in the post last month asking her which shops she visited each week and which types of breakfast cereal she had eaten over the last five years – how silly was that? So why shouldn't Harry be doing a survey about who had slept in his beds?

'Well, all I know about that bed is that it was handmade locally a few years before I was born. I should think Grandma and Grandad are the only people who've slept in it.'

'And me,' Evie pointed out. 'And you. And someone else might have slept in it too, when they came to stay.'

'I don't think Grandma would invite someone who wasn't family to sleep in her bed, Evie. That's why she had the spare room.'

Evie frowned. Her mum had a point.

'By the way,' Mum said, 'I've been meaning to ask you — how long are you planning to leave your doll's house in the middle of Grandma's dining table? I don't know why Grandma asked you to bring it. It's not as though you play with it any more.'

Evie thought she may as well tell Mum the truth about the doll's house. After all, Mum was going to find out soon enough when she saw it sitting at the bottom of the garden. 'Grandma asked me to bring it because she wanted me to put it at the bottom of her garden for the fairies to play in.'

Mum frowned. 'Evie, I'm beginning to get quite worried about you. None of your friends believe in fairies, do they?'

'No . . .' Her best friend had stopped believing in fairies quite recently when she'd woken up one night and caught her dad taking away the tooth she had left for the tooth fairy.

'So aren't you worried the other children will laugh at you, if they find out that you believe in them? Children can be very cruel sometimes . . .' Mum broke off, looking very far away all of a sudden. 'You're so trusting, Evie. You remind me of . . .' She didn't finish.

'Who?' Evie asked. 'Grandma?'

Mum shook her head. 'Never mind. What's that piece of paper for? Were you going to write a letter to someone?'

Evie looked down at the fairy letter she was still holding. It had lost its writing now that the moonlight was no longer shining on it. 'Oh, no . . . I was just going to put it away upstairs. I think I'll go to bed now. I'm quite tired.' She went over and kissed her mum goodnight.

As Evie reached the door her mother asked, 'That old bed isn't too uncomfortable for you, is it? We can always swap back again if you want.'

'Oh, no, Mum. It's fine! I sleep really well in it.'

'All right, then. Well . . . sweet dreams.'

Evie smiled, and wished her mum the same.

8

Evie woke up the next morning surprised – and quite disappointed – that Star and Moonbeam hadn't visited her during the night. She went over to the dressing table to check how many violet creams were left and found the same number as the previous day. Not that she had really expected Star and Moonbeam to come in the night without waking her up.

In the afternoon, she took two violet creams with her, wrapped up in cling film, when they went to visit Grandma. 'They're for Harry,' she explained, when her mum noticed her holding them. She wanted to give them to him so that he could leave them out for his dream fairies. That way they were sure to come back and visit him soon.

When they got to the ward, Grandma's doctor was writing in some case notes at the nurses' station and Mum went over to speak to him. Evie went straight to Harry's room but found that it was empty. At first she thought he must be having a bath or something, but when she went inside the room his bed was stripped of sheets and all his things were gone from the locker. She went back to the nurses' station to find that Mum had gone off to speak with the doctor in his office and all the nurses were busy. She stood there for what seemed like forever until one of the nurses stopped what she was doing and asked, 'Can I help?'

'I'm looking for Mr Watson.'

'Mr Watson? Oh, yes . . . He went home this morning.'

'Oh.' Evie didn't know what to say. She needed to speak to Harry and now she couldn't. She found that she was fighting back tears. She hadn't expected Harry to leave without saying goodbye to her.

'Are you Evie?' Another nurse was looking at her now.

Evie nodded.

'Harry left something for you.' She went to the other end of the long desk and came back with an envelope that had Evie's name on it.

'Thank you,' Evie said, smiling with relief. So Harry hadn't forgotten about her after all. She opened the envelope. There was a card inside and Harry had printed his address and phone number at the top of it.

Dear Evie,

Sorry I don't have time to say goodbye in person but my neighbour is coming to collect me at lunchtime. I wanted to thank you for your visits. They really cheered me up. I think your grandma is very lucky to have you as her granddaughter.

I must start packing to go home now. I can't tell you how much I am looking forward to sleeping in my own bed – and to seeing Twinkle and Sky again!

Kind regards,

Harry.

P.S. Come and see me some time if you would like to.

Without thinking, Evie showed the letter to her mother as soon as she returned from her talk with the doctor. 'I really want to go and see him, Mum. Can we go on the way back from the hospital?'

Mum shook her head. 'He'll be busy settling in at home today.' She seemed distracted. She gave the card back to Evie without even asking who Twinkle and Sky were.

In Grandma's room, Mum pulled her seat nearer to the bed and picked up Grandma's hand. 'Why don't you sit round the other side?' she said to Evie. 'I'm sure Grandma would like it if you held her hand too.' Her voice sounded a little trembly.

'Mum, is anything wrong?'

Her mother didn't reply. She just kept stroking Grandma's hand.

Evie wished Grandma would open her eyes again. She remembered all the times Grandma's eyes had crinkled up with laughter at something funny Evie had said.

She tried to think of something funny to tell her now, but she couldn't. Grandma seemed to be in a very deep sleep today in any case. 'Has Grandma still been waking up in the night?' she asked her mum.

'No.' Mum's eyes filled with tears. She looked at Evie's anxious face for a moment or two, then she rested Grandma's hand back on the bed and stood up. 'Come with me.'

She led Evie along the corridor and into the little room where the patients sometimes went to watch TV. The room was empty today and the television was switched off. Mum sat down on one of the chairs and waited until Evie was sitting too.

She spoke very softly and slowly. 'Evie, the doctor just told me that he thinks Grandma probably *won't* wake up again any more.' She was watching Evie's face carefully as if she wanted to make sure that Evie understood what she was telling her. 'He thinks she might have had another little stroke.'

Evie heard what her mother said, but felt strangely like she was being told some bad news about somebody else's grandmother. She couldn't seem to take it in.

'They don't know how much longer she's got but . . . but they don't think it'll be more than a few days,' Mum continued, gently.

'A few *days*?' Now Evie was staring at her mother in disbelief.

The shock on Evie's face was too much for Mum. As Evie continued to stare at her helplessly, Mum burst into tears.

There wasn't much time left now for Evie to turn Grandma's hospital bed into a magic one and she still didn't know how she was going to do it.

Mum spent a long time on the phone to Dad that evening. He told her that after tomorrow he was going to take a few days off and join them at Grandma's. Mum seemed to cheer up a bit after his phone call and she even suggested that she and Evie make some fairy cakes together, since Grandma had all the ingredients in her cupboard.

Evie knew Mum was trying her best to cheer her up, but her heart wasn't really in it as she got out Grandma's big mixing bowl and helped Mum weigh out the sugar and flour. While the cakes were in the oven, Mum went upstairs to have a bath and Evie decided that she couldn't wait any longer to speak to Harry. She went out into the hall and phoned the number he had written at the top of his card.

'Evie!' he exclaimed as soon as he heard

her voice. 'I didn't expect to hear from you so soon. Sorry I had to leave without saying goodbye.'

'That's all right. Harry . . . Mr Watson . . . I need your help.' She took a deep breath and started speaking very rapidly. 'It's to do with the fairies. They want to  take Grandma to fairyland in her dreams, but they can only do it if I can get together the person who made her magic bed and the three people who activated it, so that we can make her *hospital* bed magic. But I don't even know for sure if you're the person who made her bed and, even if you are, I can't find the other person who slept in it besides Grandma and me, and—'

'Slow down a minute,' Harry interrupted her. 'Firstly . . . I can easily tell if that bed is one of mine if I come and have a look at it.'

'Can you? Only you've got to do it soon because the doctor doesn't think Grandma's got much time left.'

'Oh dear . . .' Harry's voice immediately became softer. 'I *am* sorry to hear that.'

'Evie, who are you speaking to?' Mum was coming down the stairs in her dressing gown. Evie could hear the bath water still running – she'd forgotten that Grandma's bath always took ages to fill.

Evie struggled to think of a good person to pretend to be speaking to, but she couldn't. 'Harry,' she said.

'Mr Watson – from the hospital?'

Evie nodded.

'You phoned him after what I said?'

'You didn't say I couldn't *phone* him today.

You just said we couldn't *visit* him.'

In her ear Harry said, 'Let me speak to her, Evie.'

'He wants to speak to you,' she said, quickly handing the phone to her mother.

Mum went all polite then, asking Harry how he was and saying she was sure he must be glad to be home. Whatever he said in reply made her nod. 'Of course. Yes . . . Well, I'm glad she cared enough to phone you too . . . Well, that's very kind of you . . . . Our address here is 67 Churchfield Road, but . . . Oh well, in that case, Evie will be pleased to see you, I'm sure. Shall I put her back on?' She handed the phone back to Evie. 'Mr Watson is going to pop in and see you tomorrow morning. He's got something he wants to show you.' She lowered her voice to a whisper. 'It's some old photograph he's got of his shop that he thinks you'll be interested

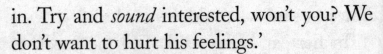

in. Try and *sound* interested, won't you? We don't want to hurt his feelings.'

Evie smiled and nodded.

'Has that done the trick?' Harry asked as soon as she got back on the phone.

'Mr Watson, have you *really* got an old photograph of your shop to show me?' Evie said, smiling as Mum gave her a thumbs-up sign of approval before going to check on the bath.

'I hope I can find one,' Harry replied, sounding a bit doubtful.

But Evie was already worrying about something else. She lowered her voice so that Mum couldn't hear. 'How are we going to find the third person who slept in Grandma's bed? My grandad didn't believe in fairies, so it can't have been him. And the only other person I know who's ever slept in that bed is my mum and she *really* doesn't believe in fairies!'

'Hmm . . . Have you asked your mother who else might have stayed in the house?'

'Yes, but she doesn't know – apart from some Canadian cousins and I really hope it isn't them. I'm hoping Star and Moonbeam will visit me tonight so I can ask *them* about it.'

'I'm not sure they'll be free to visit you tonight, Evie. Twinkle and Sky left me a welcome-home message in proper ink so I could read it straight away. They say they're having one of their emergency parties tonight to cheer up the Moon.'

'Is it blue, then?'

'Too cloudy to tell, but I presume so.'

'Star and Moonbeam didn't come and see me *last* night either,' Evie said. 'That must be why. They must've been too busy sewing sequins on their party dresses or something.'

Harry laughed. 'I'd better go . . . My daughter will be here soon. She's coming to look after me for a few days while I get my strength back, bless her. Just think, Evie, she was younger than you when I made that bed of your grandmother's.'

Evie put the phone down, trying to imagine Harry's daughter as a little girl. She found it quite difficult. She glanced at the old photograph of her mother, which Grandma kept on the hall table, and found it almost *impossible* to think of her as that little girl in pigtails and round glasses.

Evie went to bed that night not really expecting to see the fairies. So when she woke to feel her feet being tickled, she was delighted.

'Star and Moonbeam! I thought you wouldn't come tonight!'

Star flew out of the bed first and landed on Evie's pillow. She was wearing a blue party dress with blue ribbons tied around her ankles. Moonbeam was just behind her, wearing a blue sparkly dress and a sparkly pendant in the shape of a blue crescent moon.

'There's a Blue Moon party in the park tonight,' they told her. 'If we don't cheer him

up, we won't have any moonlit nights any more because he'll stay moping behind a cloud forever. We were wondering if you wanted to come.'

'Come with you to the *fairy party*?' Evie could hardly believe her luck.

'Yes. You were quite easy to shrink last time, so it won't be any trouble.'

Star was sniffing the air as if she could smell something interesting. 'Have you been *baking*?'

'Mum and I made fairy cakes. They're downstairs.'

'Cakes for us? Ooh, yummy! Can we see them?' And before Evie could point out that, despite their name, the cakes hadn't been made just for them, Star had flown out of the open bedroom door.

Evie rushed down the stairs after her, hoping Mum wouldn't hear them. 'They haven't been iced yet,' she whispered as she joined Star in the kitchen and switched on the light so they could see better. 'I was going to make pink icing tomorrow.'

'Why don't you make *blue* icing *now* – and then we can take them with us to the party?' Star said. 'We can shrink them to make them the right size.'

'Everything has to be blue at a Blue Moon party, you see,' Moonbeam explained, flying over to hover above the fairy cakes

with Star. 'All the fairies will be wearing
blue dresses. Have you got something blue
you can wear?'

'I don't think so.' Evie frowned. 'Most of
my clothes are at home.'

'That doesn't matter,' Star said. 'When
we get to Dreamland we'll lend you
something.'

'A *fairy* dress?' Evie was excited. 'Will it
be sparkly?'

'Of course. And we'll lend you some
matching fairy knickers too.'

'You'd better hurry up and ice these cakes
or they won't be ready in time,' Moonbeam
put in. 'Have you got any blue icing?'

'I can make some,' Evie replied. Grandma
had every food colouring imaginable. Evie
went into the walk-in cupboard and found
what she needed on one of the shelves. She
had mixed up icing lots of times before with

Grandma so she knew exactly what to do. The fairies watched her add water to the icing sugar and mix it together before adding a tiny amount of blue food colouring.

'That's perfect,' Moonbeam said, watching the icing take on a bright blue colour as Evie stirred the mixture.

'Now all we have to do is spread it on the cakes.'

Soon all the cakes were iced and Evie found a big tray of Grandma's to put them on.

In Grandma's bedroom, the fairies told Evie to stand in the middle of the floor with the tray so that they could shrink her – and it – before she got into bed. That way the fairy cakes wouldn't get squashed under the covers. The fairy magic happened just like before. But this time when Evie opened her eyes after being sprinkled with fairy dust she found that she was standing in the middle of Grandma's bedroom carpet, which now seemed to stretch out a very long way all around her.

Star quickly took the tray of cakes from her and flew off with it. Moonbeam took Evie's hand so they could fly inside the bed together.

As they flew along the tunnel to Dreamland, Moonbeam called ahead to Star, 'Slow down or you'll drop the cakes!'

Star clearly had her mouth full as she called back to them that the cakes were fine.

'Stop eating them!' Moonbeam shouted out crossly.

But Star had flown even further ahead by that time and it seemed like she couldn't hear.

By the time Evie and Moonbeam arrived in Dreamland, Star had already taken the cakes – minus one – to the park and returned with a blue fairy dress, which she had managed to borrow. 'One of our friends lives there,' she said, pointing to a nearby cloud house. 'I'm sure she won't mind if you go in to get changed.'

The door of the cloud house was opened by a pretty blonde fairy with a light blue dress and blue ribbons in her hair. Star introduced her as Twinkle.

'Are you Harry's friend?' Evie asked her.

'That's right. Do you know him? I visit him with Sky. She lives here too but she's already gone to the party because she's playing in the orchestra.'

'Twinkle, can we come inside so that Evie can change into her party dress?' Moonbeam asked.

'Of course.' Twinkle led them into a room that had white walls made entirely of cloud. There was a lovely sofa made of cloud too, which had a pink cover thrown over it. The table and chairs were made out of beams of light just like the ones in Queen Celeste's palace. Several photographs hung in frames around the room – mostly photographs of fairies – but Evie noticed there was also one of Harry. 'He's our best human friend,' Twinkle said, seeing her looking at it, 'so we took a picture of him. I'll take one of you too, if you like, when you're wearing your fairy dress.' She went off to fetch her camera and Star said that Evie had better hurry up and get changed because the party had already started. She showed Evie into one of the fairy bedrooms and told her to call out if she needed any help.

Evie took off her pyjamas and put them on the cloud bed. Then she put on the blue sparkly dress and matching knickers – which both fitted her perfectly now that she was fairy-sized herself. There was a mirror on one wall and when she went to look at herself she couldn't help smiling – she looked so pretty. Now all she had to do was fix her hair.

Twinkle lent her a moon-shaped hairbrush and some blue sparkly ribbon. 'If you had wings you'd look exactly like a fairy,' she said. 'Shall I take a photo of you with Star and Moonbeam?'

The fairy camera was a gold box with a big star on the front of it that slid up and down like a shutter when it was taking a picture. 'It's got fairy dust inside it,' Twinkle explained.

'Can you take a photo for us too?' Star and Moonbeam asked.

'Of course.'

'Can I have one?' Evie said, thinking how cool it would be to have a photograph of her with the fairies, to show all her friends.

But this time Twinkle shook her head. 'I'm afraid you can't take fairy photographs out of fairyland,' she explained. 'It's against the fairy rules.'

'You can have a fairy goody bag to take home with you instead,' Moonbeam put in quickly. 'We always get great goody bags at the end of our parties.'

'What's in a fairy goody bag?'

'Something different every time, so you'll have to wait and see.'

'OK, everyone . . .' Twinkle was putting down her camera. 'If we're all ready, I'll go and fetch the shoe dust.'

'*Shoe* dust?' Evie looked at Moonbeam.

'It's a special type of fairy dust,' Moonbeam explained. 'You'll see in a minute.'

Twinkle came back into the room holding a round box with a pink lid and a handle in the shape of a gold high-heeled shoe. She carefully took the lid off the box and took out a handful of gold-coloured dust. She sprinkled some over Star's bare feet, and Star's toes immediately began to sparkle. Suddenly a glittering blue shoe – decorated with a shiny blue star – appeared on each foot.

'Wow!' Evie exclaimed. 'That's amazing!

But I thought you said Queen Celeste didn't let you use fairy dust to make clothes.'

'Oh, she feels differently about shoes,' Star replied. 'And this way we only ever own one pair at a time. Otherwise our houses would be full of them!'

Twinkle gave the shoe dust to Moonbeam – who got shiny blue shoes with moon-shaped buckles on them – before sprinkling some over Evie's feet.

'It feels tickly,' Evie said as she watched her own toes sparkle. Then *she* was wearing sparkly shoes too, which were very grown-up looking and matched her dress exactly.

Last of all, Twinkle sprinkled her own feet to produce a very smart pair of blue and silver shoes with blue bows at the front.

'How long will the magic last for?' Evie asked, feeling a bit like Cinderella in her magic party outfit. What if the magic wore off before the end of the party and she was left wearing nothing at all?

'The clothes won't vanish – don't worry. And the shoes will only disappear if you take them off,' Star replied.

'But what if I need to take them off to give my feet a rest?' Evie asked. Her mum was always taking off her shoes to give her feet a rest in the middle of parties, especially if they were new shoes. She said it was because new shoes nearly always pinched your feet. And these shoes looked much more like the kind of shoes her mum wore than the kind she normally wore herself.

'Fairy shoes *never* hurt your feet,' Moonbeam reassured her, 'even if you dance in them all night. So you won't need to take them off.'

'Come on,' Star said, opening the front door. 'We don't want to miss all the food, do we?'

The three fairies led Evie to the park where the Blue Moon party was already in full swing. Evie thought it was beautiful. The whole park was lit up with blue fairy lights, and fairies were dancing in blue dresses and sitting at little tables that had blue tablecloths on them with blue candles in the centre. Blue balloons were hanging from the trees or floating about in bunches, tied together with blue ribbon. A fairy orchestra was playing lively dance music, and sitting right at the front was the fairy Evie had seen before with the harp. Twinkle pointed out a pretty fairy who was playing a blue violin and said proudly, 'That's Sky. She's a very good violinist. She tried to give

Harry lessons once, but he made such a din that his neighbour started banging on the wall.'

A long table was laid out with fairy food. Evie noticed her fairy cakes with their blue icing, and beside them a really huge cake which had blue icing that sparkled. 'That's one of your cakes too,' Star told her. 'We used a bit of fairy dust to reverse the shrinking. That way we can give a slice to everyone.' There were plates of blue cloud tarts, mini blueberry muffins and magic fruit biscuits that had been sprinkled with blue hundreds-and-thousands. There were bottles of blue fizzy drink too and blue glasses to drink from.

'Will the Moon actually *come* to the party?' Evie asked, looking out into the Night Sky and seeing only stars.

'See that big cloud over there?'

Moonbeam said, pointing. 'He's hiding behind that. He can see us, though, and later on, when he's cheered up, he'll come out.'

Evie was unsure how anyone could be cheered up by a party they weren't actually at.

Moonbeam explained it to her. 'He watches us down here having all this fun, dancing in our blue dresses and eating our blue party food. Then he sees how pretty the blue fairy lights are – and the blue candles and the blue balloons. And after a while he looks at himself, and instead of feeling depressed because he's blue, he starts to think that blue is actually a very nice colour. So he starts to feel much better about himself and he stops feeling sad and comes out from behind his cloud. Then, because he's not sad, he goes back to being his normal brilliant-white colour. And then he's so happy that he usually starts humming.'

'*Humming?*'

'Yes.'

Just then the music stopped abruptly and all the fairies stopped chattering. Everyone was looking in the direction of a platform where Queen Celeste was standing on a blue carpet, wearing a stunning blue dress that was trimmed with blue raindrops. On her feet she wore a pair of very stylish, high-heeled, pointy-toed blue-and-gold shoes. 'Let the fireworks begin!' she announced grandly, reaching upwards with her wand, which had a sparkling blue star at the end of it.

With that, there was a loud bang and a shower of blue shooting stars lit up the sky. More fireworks followed until the sky was totally filled with blue stars of all different sizes, which fizzed and banged and sparkled as the fairies watched.

'There he is!' several fairies shouted at

once. Everyone clapped as the Moon emerged from behind his cloud. In a matter of seconds he was no longer blue but had returned to his normal bright colour. All the fairies cheered loudly and Evie joined in.

At the end of the party two fairies stood at the park gates giving everyone a party bag to take home with them. Evie couldn't wait to see what was in hers and she opened it as soon as they got back to Twinkle's house. Inside was a tiny pot of shoe dust, a miniature bottle of fairy perfume, a pink pen with a star on the end of it, which lit up when you wrote, and some pink and yellow sweets that had Evie's name written on them. Evie saw that the fairies each had sweets with *their* names on them too.

'Can I really take these things home with me?' she asked, spraying some fairy perfume on her wrist and nearly sneezing because it had rather a strong smell.

'Yes. The shoe dust won't work outside Fairyland, but it *is* real so take good care of it. You might want to use it if you ever visit us again.'

'I've had such a wonderful time!' Evie gasped. 'Thank you so much for inviting me!' She suddenly felt very sleepy. She couldn't help yawning.

'The Moon is humming us all to sleep now,' Moonbeam told her, yawning loudly herself. 'He always does that after we've thrown him a good party.' She opened the window so they could hear better, and Evie heard that the tune the Moon was humming was the fairy lullaby.

'Come and lie down on the sofa,' Twinkle suggested. 'It's very comfortable. You'll be asleep in no time.'

Evie did as Twinkle said, kicking off her fairy shoes and watching them sparkle for an instant before disappearing. Then she closed her eyes, knowing that when she woke up again she would be back in Grandma's brass bed.

Evie was waiting at the window when Harry arrived with his daughter the next morning. Mum was on the phone talking to Dad again and she nodded when Evie said she was going to open the front door. Evie could hear her telling Dad she'd ring him back later.

'I found that old photograph I was telling you about,' Harry said, winking at her.

Mum came to greet them and asked Harry and Margaret to sit down while she went to put the kettle on. 'We should have some fairy cakes to offer you too, but I'm not sure where Evie's put them.'

Evie flushed. 'They . . . er . . . they aren't here any more.'

'What do you mean?'

'I iced them but they didn't turn out like I'd expected.' Evie thought of the tiny fairy-sized cakes that she had taken to the fairy party. 'I sort of gave them away.'

'Gave them away? Who to?'

Fortunately, Harry seemed to realize what the problem was and he came to her rescue. 'To the birds, I expect, was it, Evie? That's what I always do with my cooking when it doesn't turn out right. I give it to our winged friends out there and they always seem to enjoy it.'

Evie nodded. After all, she *had* given the cakes to her winged friends, hadn't she?

Mum was shaking her head. 'I don't know why you didn't wait for me to help you ice them, Evie. They were perfectly all right when I took them out of the oven last night.'

'Sorry,' Evie muttered, as Mum went off, a little huffily, into the kitchen.

'I hear you might be sleeping in one of Dad's brass beds, Evie,' Margaret said, smiling at her. 'It's amazing that it's still in one piece after all these years.'

'Of course it's still in one piece!' Harry scowled at his daughter. '*My* beds were made to last.'

'Why don't you come upstairs now and have a look at it?' Evie invited him.

Harry stood up straight away but Margaret replied, 'I think we'd better check that's OK with your mum first, Evie. She might not want Dad going tramping all over her house.'

'It's not *her* house, it's Grandma's house,' Evie said. She shouted through to her mother in the kitchen, 'Mum, you don't mind if I take Harry up and show him Grandma's bed, do you? He wants to see if it's one of the ones *he* made.'

Mum came back into the room. 'Well, I don't know how tidy it is up there.'

'It's fine,' Evie said, heading for the door.

'Evie, what about the photograph Mr Watson brought to show you? Have you had a look at it yet?'

'I'm just going to, but he really wants to see the bed first.'

'Sentimental value, you know,' Harry put in quickly. 'I reckon it's probably one of the first beds I ever made.' He looked at his daughter. 'You used to love coming and watching me in my workshop. Do you remember?'

'Of course. You used to let me polish the brass bed knobs as a special treat. Child labour, I call it!'

Harry chuckled. Mum smiled too. She told Evie she could take Harry upstairs and that she would sit down with Margaret and wait for the kettle to boil.

As soon as Harry walked into Grandma's bedroom and saw the bed, he smiled. 'It's one of mine all right.' He went over and tenderly touched the bed-frame as if he was greeting an old friend. He walked around it for several minutes, admiring it, and it seemed to Evie as if he had temporarily forgotten why he was really there.

'So if this *is* a bed that you made,' she said pointedly, 'then all we have to do is find the third person who slept in it.' She frowned. 'But I still don't know who that could be.'

Harry was about to say something when he noticed the tiny goody bag on Evie's bedside table. 'I see the fairies have been leaving you presents.'

Evie nodded. 'I was going to tell you about it. The fairies took me to their Blue Moon party last night and I met Twinkle and Sky. I went to Twinkle's house and she had a photograph of you up on her wall.'

'Never!' Harry looked amazed. 'A photo of *me*?'

'Yes. Don't you remember her taking it?'

'I remember her messing around with that funny camera thing when she came to visit me one night, but she said she couldn't tell if the picture would come out until she got back to fairyland.'

'Well, it did. It's a really nice one too.'

Margaret was calling up to them that the tea was made, so they went back downstairs.

'Did you make my mother's bed then, Mr Watson?' Mum asked, as Harry sat down beside Margaret on the sofa.

'I certainly did.'

'A lot of work must have gone into it.'

Harry nodded. 'I worked all on my own, too, in the early days. Later I got an assistant to help me, but I was on my own when I made that one.'

'Well, it's certainly lasted my mother a good long time,' Mum said. 'It must be forty years old at least.'

'It should have been comfortable too. I only used the best mattresses, you see – that's very important when you're making a quality bed.'

Mum smiled and Evie wondered if she was going to tell the truth about how uncomfortable *she* found Grandma's bed. But instead she replied, politely, 'I used to love sleeping in it when I was little. My parents weren't ones to let me sneak into bed with them much, but I remember once when I had pneumonia I got to sleep in it with my mother for a whole week because she was so worried about me.' She leaned forwards towards the coffee table. 'We'd better drink our tea before it gets cold.' She picked up a mug and handed it to Harry.

Grandma would have made them tea in a pot, with a milk jug and a sugar bowl and proper cups and saucers, Evie thought, and she would have laid the biscuits out on a plate whereas Mum had just plonked the packet on the table. The biscuits were ones Mum had chosen, with currants in them. Grandma wouldn't have liked those biscuits, Evie thought, because the currants would have got stuck in her teeth.

'How long are you staying with your father?' Mum asked Margaret.

'A few days, I hope. If Dad'll have me that long.'

'I think I can *just* about put up with you,'

Harry joked, but he looked pleased really.

Mum asked if Harry had any other children and he shook his head. 'I was one of eight and my wife was one of twelve – so we decided Margaret was enough for us!'

Mum laughed. 'I'm an only one too.'

'So am I,' Evie said. 'But once I made up a pretend sister, didn't I, Mum?'

Mum nodded, smiling at her. 'When Evie was little, she had an imaginary sister called Angelina. Angelina had to come everywhere with us, didn't she, Evie? Evie used to get very cross when people sat on her on buses!' Mum smiled. 'Mind you, *I'm* one to talk. I had an imaginary friend when I was little too.'

'Did you?' This was news to Evie. 'What was she called?'

'Buttercup.'

'*Buttercup?*'

Evie hardly spoke for the rest of the time Harry and his daughter were there – except to pretend to be interested in the very blurry black-and-white photo Harry eventually produced, which showed the front of his shop forty years ago. Evie couldn't wait to ask Mum if her imaginary friend was the same Buttercup that Grandma had told her about. But if so, that meant Mum's friend had been a fairy. And how could she be, when Mum didn't believe in fairies?

As soon as their guests had left and they were alone together, Evie asked, 'Mum, was Buttercup a *fairy*?'

Mum nodded. 'How did you guess?'

'But I thought you didn't believe in fairies?'

Mum didn't answer for a few moments. She looked as though she was thinking very carefully about something. 'I *did* believe in fairies when I was your age,' she finally replied, 'and it got me into a lot of trouble. That's why I get so cross when Grandma tells *you* that fairies are real.' She sat down on the sofa beside Evie. 'The thing is . . . I must have had a very active imagination when I was little, because I truly thought I saw a fairy in a yellow dress in our back garden. Grandma encouraged me by telling me how my fairy sounded just like a fairy called Buttercup whom she had met herself a few times. She even showed me a dried-flower bracelet that she'd pressed inside a book, which she said Buttercup had given her as a present. Of course, I kept imagining I saw Buttercup all over the place after that and I used to leave out treats for her at night, which were always gone in the morning. Then I made the mistake of taking the flower bracelet to school to show everybody. Some of the children used to tease me because I wore glasses, you see, and I thought they'd stop teasing me when they knew I had a friend who was a real fairy. But they made fun of me even more after that. They said I was a baby to believe in fairies because everyone knew that there was no such thing. They made my life at school miserable. Even the nicer children didn't dare try to be friends with me in case they got picked on too. I was very lonely for a while.'

'That's terrible!' Evie gasped, hating to think of her mum being so unhappy at school. 'Couldn't Grandma do anything about it?' Mum had always told Evie that if ever *she* was being bullied, she must tell her mum or dad straight away.

'I didn't tell Grandma how bad things were. I just told her I didn't want to wear my glasses and that I wasn't going to believe in fairies any more because nobody else at school believed in them. Grandma said I had no choice about the glasses and that fairies were a fact, no matter what anybody else believed. She was wrong, though. Soon after that my eyesight improved, so I stopped needing the glasses. And as for fairies being real, all I know is that as soon as I decided to stop believing in them, I never saw one again. Gradually the other children stopped teasing me and my life at school got easier.'

'But you *never* saw Buttercup again?'

'No. Like I said, I think she must have been a sort of imaginary friend, like your Angelina.'

'But you actually *saw* Buttercup. I never really saw Angelina.'

'I think having Grandma telling me so

often that Buttercup was real made me think I'd actually *seen* her, when I can't have done. And that's why I worry when Grandma talks so much about fairies to *you*, Evie. I couldn't bear for you to go through what I did.'

'There aren't any bullies in my class, Mum,' Evie said, 'so don't worry about me. Anyway, a few of the other girls at school *do* believe in fairies too. I'm not the only one.'

'Really?' Mum looked sceptical.

'Yes.' Evie was almost bursting to ask her next question. 'So when you were little and you believed in fairies, was that when you slept in Grandma's bed?'

Mum looked puzzled. 'How do you mean?'

'Did you ever sleep in Grandma's bed at the same time that you believed in fairies?' Evie repeated impatiently.

'Well, I suppose I must have done. But what a strange question. Why do you want to know that?'

But Evie decided it was best not to try to explain. The main thing was that she now knew the identity of the third person who had activated the bed's magic. It was Mum!

When Evie phoned Harry and told him what she had discovered, he promised to come to the hospital at visiting time that afternoon. He said he had just bought a box of violet creams for the fairies, but he would tell Margaret they were for the nurses, and that way he could get her to drive him up to the hospital.

So that afternoon, when Harry put his head round the door of Grandma's room, Evie pretended to be surprised to see him.

Harry quickly explained to Mum that he had come back to the ward with a gift for the staff. 'How is she?' he asked, coming to stand on Mum's side of the bed.

'She doesn't seem to be in any discomfort,' Mum replied, looking tenderly at Grandma, whose face seemed to be getting thinner and less like Grandma's face every day. Mum was already holding one of Grandma's hands so Evie quickly picked up the other one and reached across the bed to take Harry's.

'Let's all hold hands for a minute,' Evie said. 'Mum, you and Harry hold hands too and then we can . . . we can . . .' She was put off finishing by the look Mum was giving her – as if she thought Evie had gone a little mad.

'What a lovely idea!' Harry said quickly, taking Mum's hand before she could protest.

Evie held her breath. They were all linked up now – Harry, who had made Grandma's magic bed, and the three people who had activated it, Evie, Mum and Grandma. They were doing just what Queen Celeste had instructed them to do – holding hands together around the new bed – and any second now the bed should become magical.

Evie waited for something to happen – for the bed to start sparkling like Queen Celeste had told her it would – but everything just stayed the same. Evie couldn't understand it. She looked across at Harry in dismay.

'What's wrong?' Mum asked, seeing the look on Evie's face and letting go of Harry's hand.

'Nothing,' Evie replied, letting go too and stepping backwards away from the bed.

'I'd better go. Margaret's waiting for me

in the car,' Harry said. 'Why don't you walk along the corridor with me a little way, Evie?'

As soon as they were out of earshot of Mum, Evie asked, 'Why do you think it didn't work?'

'Maybe it did. Maybe there's nothing to see when a bed becomes magical.'

'Queen Celeste said that the bed would sparkle as the magic reaction took place.'

Harry frowned. 'Well, I don't know what went wrong then.'

Suddenly Evie thought of something. 'Do you think it's because Mum doesn't believe in fairies any more? Do you think that's why the magic didn't work?'

Harry frowned again. 'I just don't know, Evie. Why don't you ask your fairy friends about it tonight? I'll certainly ask my two if they come and see me – though I'm not sure they will, since I've given their chocolates away to those nurses now. I'd better buy some more before I go home.' And as Evie went back to the ward, Harry went to see if the hospital shop had any violet creams left or, failing that, chocolate raisins, which he knew were Twinkle and Sky's second-favourite kind of chocolate.

11

Evie left what remained of her own violet creams on her pillow that night with a note attached saying, *Dear Star and Moonbeam, Please wake me up as soon as you get here. I need to speak to you URGENTLY!*

Then she did her best to drop off to sleep, but she was so tensed up that it was very difficult. She tried to count sheep to make herself sleepy but that didn't work. Then, just as she was giving up hope of ever falling asleep, a familiar tune suddenly popped into her head. It was the fairy lullaby she had heard in Queen Celeste's palace – and again at the end of the Blue Moon party – and as she remembered it and started to hum it to herself she found herself drifting off.

When she next woke up, her fairy friends were sitting on her pillow. 'Star! Moonbeam! Thank goodness you're here!' she burst out, sitting up abruptly and turning on her bedside lamp.

The two fairies blinked in the brightness. They had been trying to read her note and eat a violet cream at the same time, with only the light of their fairy lanterns to help them.

Evie quickly told them what had happened at the hospital. 'I don't understand why the fairy magic didn't work, because I got everyone together just like Queen Celeste said. The only reason I can think of is that my mum doesn't believe in fairies any more. Would that make a difference?'

'She *did* believe in fairies when she *slept* in the bed, didn't she?' Star asked.

'Yes. She actually *saw* a fairy called Buttercup when she was little, but now she thinks she was just imagining her.'

'It shouldn't make any difference what she thinks now,' Moonbeam said. 'Once you've believed in fairies, you never really stop.'

'Mum has.'

Moonbeam shook her head. 'She might *think* she has, but there'll always be some doubt in her mind, no matter how hard she tries to tell herself otherwise.'

Evie wasn't sure that was true but she decided not to waste time arguing about it. 'Why didn't the magic work then?'

'There must have been someone missing,' Moonbeam said.

'But we were all there: the person who made Grandma's magic bed – that's Harry – and the three people who activated it – Grandma, Mum and me.'

'Were *all* the people who made the bed there?' Moonbeam asked.

'Harry made it by himself. He didn't have anyone helping him. He told me that.'

Star flew over to the bed and balanced herself on one of the bed knobs. 'He put this huge thing together all by himself?'

'It's not that huge, Star,' Evie said. 'Not if you're human-sized.'

Star was trying to do a pirouette on the bed knob. As Evie watched her, she suddenly remembered something. 'Harry's daughter said that when she was a little girl she used to polish the bed knobs. That wouldn't have counted as *making* the bed, would it?'

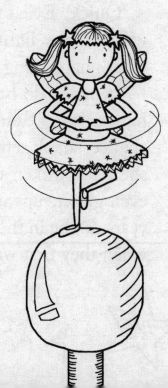

'Of course it would!' Moonbeam exclaimed, jumping up. 'Polish is a very important part of a brass bed.'

'But she doesn't believe in fairies any more than—' Evie broke off. She had been going to say, 'any more than Mum does'. But what about when Margaret was little? Had she believed in fairies then?

The sound of the telephone ringing made them all jump.

'Quick!' Evie said. 'You'd better go. Mum will see the lights and come to find out what's happening.'

'It might do her good to find out what's happening,' Star said. 'There's a good chance she'll actually be able to see us if she's just woken up. It's a funny thing, but even grown-ups who haven't seen a fairy in years can be in the right mind for seeing one when they first wake up.'

Evie heard Mum's bedroom door opening and saw the landing light go on. Then she heard her go down to the hall and pick up the phone. She could tell from Mum's side of the conversation that it was the hospital at the other end. She felt her insides go tight. They must be phoning about Grandma.

She completely forgot about Star and Moonbeam as she went out on to the landing and sat on the top stair to hear better. Mum was saying she would get a taxi and come to the hospital straight away.

'Is Grandma worse?' she asked, as soon as Mum put down the phone.

'Evie, you're awake . . .' Mum paused. 'Yes, darling. I'm afraid she is. She's not breathing so well and the doctor thinks I ought to go in. I can't leave you here, so I'm afraid you'll have to come too. I'm going to phone for a taxi and we'll both need to get dressed as quickly as we can.'

Evie said she was going to fetch a drink of water and waited in the kitchen until Mum had phoned the taxi firm and gone back upstairs. She was thinking very rapidly. If Grandma had got worse then there was no time to lose. She had to phone Harry and ask him to come to the hospital tonight. And he had to bring Margaret with him. She picked up Harry's card from the mantlepiece and went out to the hall to phone him.

'Evie, who are you calling?' Mum shouted to her from the landing before she could even finish punching in Harry's number.

Evie put down the phone quickly. She knew Mum would have a fit if she found out she was calling Harry at this time of night. 'I wanted to speak to . . . to . . .' She broke off.

'Were you phoning Dad?' Mum asked. 'I was just wishing he was here myself. But he can't do anything from where he is, so I don't think we should wake him up yet. I'll ring him later from the hospital. He's driving down here in the morning in any case.'

Evie went back up to her room to get dressed, wondering if she would get a chance to phone Harry from the hospital. To her surprise she found that Star and Moonbeam were still in her room. They wanted to know if they could do anything to help. At first Evie shook her head, thinking it was a silly question – after all, they'd already told her that fairies couldn't interfere in human matters of life and death, hadn't they? But then she thought of something. 'Could you get a message to Harry for me? Twinkle and Sky will know where to find him. I need them to tell him what's happened and that he has to meet me at the hospital tonight with his daughter. Tell him the magic won't work unless his daughter's there too.'

The fairies promised that they would do their best and they flew away quickly under the covers of Grandma's bed. It was only then that Evie remembered that, if her plan worked, all the magic would be transferred from this bed to Grandma's hospital bed and she wouldn't be visited by Star and Moonbeam ever again. And she hadn't even said goodbye to them.

Before she could think any more about it, Mum called for her to hurry up because their taxi would be there soon.

On the way to the hospital, Mum looked like she was trying not to cry. 'I think this might be it, darling,' Mum said, clutching her hand, 'so we're both going to have to be very brave.'

Evie hung her head, feeling terrible. What if there wasn't enough time now to get Grandma to fairyland?

The hospital felt very different at night. The corridors were dimly lit and empty, and on Grandma's ward the only bright light came from the nurses' station. A nurse was sitting with Grandma. A light was on above the bed and Evie looked at Grandma nervously. Her forehead was shiny white, her cheeks were sucked in and her breathing sounded loud.

'Let me get you a cup of tea,' the nurse said, standing up. 'The duty doctor's on the ward if you want to speak to her.'

Evie didn't really want to be left alone with Grandma, so she felt quite relieved when Mum asked her to wait in the TV room while she spoke to the doctor. When Mum came back, she told Evie gently that

Grandma was very ill now and that she might not make it through the night.

'I don't really want you to have to stay here all night with me, Evie. I wish there was someone I could leave you with.'

'It's OK,' Evie said. 'I want to be here.'

'Well, if you get tired, I'm sure the nurses won't mind you lying down in here. We could pull two of those big chairs together and get you a blanket. I think I might phone Dad after all and ask him to set off now if he can. Then he can take you back to Grandma's with him when he gets here.'

After Mum had made the call to Dad, who said he would set off right away, they went back to sit in Grandma's room together. Mum took Grandma's hand and leaned against the side of the bed as if she wanted to get as close to her as possible. Evie sat opposite her and held Grandma's other hand. She didn't hold out much hope now that Harry and Margaret would arrive in time to do anything. And even if they did, she doubted Mum would let them all hold hands around Grandma's bed now that Grandma was as ill as this.

Evie's eyes felt very tired and she must have nodded off, because the next thing she knew, Mum was slumped over with her head resting on the edge of the bed, her hand still touching Grandma's. A noise in the doorway made Evie turn and there was Harry, one finger pressed against his lips to warn her to be quiet.

She jumped up and hurried across to him. 'You came!' she whispered excitedly. 'Did the fairies give you my message?'

Harry was looking over his shoulder as if he expected to be pounced on by a nurse at any minute. He beckoned Evie out of the room and away from the door. 'The fairies did give me your message, yes, and I had a heck of a job persuading Margaret to bring me here. I had to threaten to call a taxi before she would. How's your grandmother?'

'Not very good. Listen, the reason the magic didn't work before was because Margaret wasn't here. She helped make the bed by polishing the brass knobs. She must have believed in fairies when she did that. She's got to come and hold hands with us around Grandma's bed too if we want to make it magical.'

Harry frowned. 'Of course . . . I'd forgotten about those bed knobs . . . But this is going to be tricky, Evie. Margaret doesn't think we should be here at all. Says it's interfering. She wouldn't even come into the ward with me. She's waiting out in the corridor.'

'What if *I* go and ask her to help us?'

'I don't know what she'll say. She hasn't believed in fairies in a long time.'

'I'll go and speak to her anyway,' Evie said.

She found Margaret sitting on one of the plastic seats just outside the entrance to the ward. She was yawning loudly and still looked half asleep. Remembering what Star and Moonbeam had said about grown-ups often being in the right mind to believe in fairies when they'd just woken up, Evie felt encouraged. 'Margaret . . . I need you to come with me to help Grandma. '

'Evie!' Margaret stood up. 'Are you all right?'

'Yes,' Evie replied. 'But come and see my grandma. Please.'

'But, Evie . . . Dad and I aren't family.'

'That doesn't matter. There's no one else who can do this.'

'Do *what*, Evie?'

'I'll show you.' Evie put on her most pleading expression. '*Please* come.'

Reluctantly, Margaret went with her, looking increasingly unsure that she was doing the right thing as Evie led her through the ward.

Harry was waiting for them outside Grandma's room. 'Now listen,' he said before Margaret or Evie had time to speak, '*you* might not believe in fairies, Margaret, but Evie's grandma does. And so does Evie. And Evie wants to make a fairy ring for her as a very special goodbye present. A fairy ring has to have five people in it – five people who've seen a fairy. And that's why she needs us. Isn't that right, Evie?'

Evie nodded, gazing at Harry in admiration. She was sure she couldn't have made up such a good story so quickly.

Margaret was staring at her father as if she wasn't sure how to react to what he'd just said. 'That's all very well, Dad,' she replied, frowning, 'but what does Evie's mother say about this?'

Evie had to admit that she had a point. If Mum didn't agree to them doing this, they might as well forget it. There was nothing for it now but to wake Mum up and ask her.

Inside Grandma's room, Mum was already awake. She was sitting up, rubbing her neck. 'Evie, are you all right? Where have you been?'

'I went to speak to Harry and Margaret.'

'Harry and Margaret? What are they doing here?'

'I asked them to come. You see . . .' Evie repeated to her mother more or less what Harry had just told Margaret about the fairy ring. Then she held her breath nervously as she waited for Mum to react in the way she normally did whenever fairies were mentioned.

But since Mum had only just woken up, her common sense hadn't fully kicked in yet.

At least, Evie assumed that was the reason why she gave a wry smile and said, 'So Grandma *still* has you all fired up about fairies – even now. It's amazing really. And apparently *I* can't escape either. I just dreamt about Buttercup – my fairy friend from when I was little.'

'Did you?' Evie wondered for a second if Grandma's bed had somehow already become magical. But then she reminded herself that flower fairies didn't visit you in that sort of way. Mum must have just had a normal dream about Buttercup. 'Mum, we have to make this fairy ring for Grandma while there's still time,' she persisted. 'Please, Mum. Grandma really needs us to do this for her.'

Mum reached out and gently touched Evie's anxious face. 'It seems to me that you're the one who really needs to do this,

Evie. But you're right . . .' She glanced across at her mother. 'I expect Grandma would be tickled pink at the idea of a fairy ring in her honour.' She paused. 'All right, then . . . So long as you realize that no fairy ring is going to make Grandma better.'

'I know that,' Evie said firmly.

Evie quickly invited Harry and Margaret into the room, before Mum could change her mind. She instructed everybody to link hands around Grandma's bed, and this time, as soon as they did, the whole bed began to sparkle.

12

As Mum and Margaret tried to make sense of what they'd just seen – and soon concluded that it must have been a trick of the light, since they both had much more common sense than fairy sense – Harry and Evie watched Grandma closely. On the outside, at least, she didn't seem any different.

Harry asked if Evie would like to come home with him and Margaret until her parents were ready to collect her. That way, when Dad arrived, he'd be able to stay at the hospital and support Mum. Evie shook her head at first, saying she didn't want to leave Grandma, but then Harry reminded her –

whispering so that the others wouldn't hear
– that there was a magic bed at his house
too. 'I'll sleep downstairs on the couch,' he
said, 'and you can borrow my bed.'

Evie immediately realized what he was
getting at. Now that the magic had been
transferred from Grandma's old bed to her
new one, Evie didn't have a magic bed of
her own any more. But she could still get to
Dreamland – and meet Grandma there – if
she borrowed Harry's.

So Evie agreed to go home with Harry
and Margaret.

As Evie went to kiss her grandmother
goodbye, Mum was watching her closely,
making sure she knew that this was a
forever goodbye. Evie did say her forever
goodbye to the Grandma who was lying in
front of her now, but at the same time she
knew that her last goodbye to the

Grandma she had known all her life was going to come later.

Back at Harry's house, Margaret thought it strange that her father was giving up his bed for Evie and she didn't really like the idea of him sleeping on the couch. But Harry was insistent. As Margaret tucked Evie up in Harry's big brass bed, which was almost exactly like Grandma's, Evie wished she could tell her why she needed to sleep there.

Evie didn't feel very tired at first because she was so nervous and excited at the same time, but once she closed her eyes and started to hum the fairy lullaby to herself she soon found herself in Dreamland.

Star and Moonbeam were there to greet her. They were dressed in short fluffy dresses that seemed to be made out of yellow cloud. Instead of being in bed, Evie was lying in a yellow silk hammock in a strange garden, swinging gently between two trees. She was her normal size compared to the fairies and everything in the garden seemed human-sized too. Yellow blossom had fallen on to her tummy and when Evie looked up she saw that each tree was covered in yellow petals. Instead of the borrowed T-shirt that she had gone to sleep in, she was wearing a yellow summer dress that had been a favourite of Grandma's a year or two ago. It had become too small for her eventually and Mum had given it away to a charity shop, but now it seemed to be just the right size.

'You aren't really awake this time,' the fairies told her. 'You're in our dream garden. It's yellow because that's your grandma's favourite colour and you're in her dream now. She got here before you did. She's waiting for you in the dreamkeeper's cottage.'

Evie could hardly wait to see Grandma

again. She climbed out of the hammock and Star and Moonbeam led her across a lawn of fresh green grass bordered by lovely yellow flowers. A familiar smell was coming from the little cottage – which had yellow smoke coming from its chimney this time – and when Evie stepped in through the back door, she found herself in a replica of Grandma's kitchen at home. Judging by the

smell, Grandma had been baking. There was a ginger cake resting on a wire rack on the side and a tray was laid for tea in the middle of the big kitchen table.

'I thought we'd have tea in the garden, darling,' Grandma said, stepping out from the pantry, holding her best china plate. 'What do you think?'

Seeing Grandma as she had been before her stroke, and actually hearing her voice again, brought a lump to Evie's throat. She ran forward and hugged her really tightly. She found that she was crying. 'I've missed you so much!'

Grandma hugged her close for a while, then brought out one of her yellow hankies and got Evie to dry her eyes. 'We have to have a talk,' she said, 'but let's take the tea things out first, shall we? Look, I've got all our favourite things here – chocolate cake and ginger cake and jam tarts for you and lemon-curd tarts for me.'

Evie sniffed and did her best to feel happy so as not to spoil things. 'Do you like lemon-curd tarts because your favourite colour is yellow?' she asked as they sat down in the garden together.

Grandma laughed. 'Mostly what I like about them is the taste. You know me – I've always had a sweet tooth!' Grandma was sitting in the same way as Evie, with both legs tucked round to one side. Evie had never seen her sit like that before and when she pointed it out, Grandma chuckled.

'This is my dream garden, isn't it? Do you think I'm going to choose to have eighty-year-old legs here when I can have the legs of a young girl?' She bit into a lemon-curd tart and smiled. 'I've got my own teeth back too. You don't mind if I change that chocolate cake to a fruit cake, do you? I haven't been able to eat cake with currants for years because of those wretched false teeth.'

Evie said she didn't mind as she cut herself a slice of ginger cake. 'I don't suppose I'll ever taste your ginger cake again after this, will I?' That thought made her feel very sad.

Grandma smiled. 'We'll see about that. All my cakes are made from recipes and when I'm gone those recipes will still be here. Why don't you and Mum have a go at making them? You'll find my recipe book on the kitchen shelf at home.'

'But, Grandma, I don't want you to go.' Evie was frowning.

'Evie, remember what I told you that day when we went for our walk together in the graveyard? About how I'd hate to drag on for years, not being able to look after myself?'

Evie nodded.

'Well, if I don't die now, then I *will* drag on and that won't be very nice for me, will it?'

'No, but—'

'And I am eighty, after all. It's not like I haven't had a good long life, is it?'

'Yes, but . . .' Evie frowned as she struggled to find the right words. 'But *I* haven't had you for eighty years. I've only had you for *nine*.'

Grandma sighed and for the first time she looked sad herself. 'I know you're not ready to lose me yet, darling. Neither is your mother. I'm sorry about that.'

'I know it's not your fault,' Evie said quickly, not wanting Grandma to feel bad. 'I know you can't *help* dying.'

'No, I can't.' Grandma looked at her with great fondness. 'Oh, Evie, I'm so lucky to have had you as my granddaughter. You've always made me very happy. You know that, don't you?'

Evie nodded. 'Except . . . except I think you might have missed me a lot too, when I wasn't there.'

Grandma looked surprised. 'Of course I missed you. But I knew you couldn't be with me all the time. You had to be at home with your mum and dad too, and with your friends, and at school. And I know you never forgot about me. The most important thing is this . . . from now on, you'll always remember me and I'll always remember you. Isn't that right?'

Evie's mouth felt dry and tears were welling up in her eyes, but she nodded.

'Good. Now let's go for a walk, shall we?

196

There are some things I want to show you.'

They walked through an archway in the hedge, which had moonflowers growing round it, into a field with a narrow footpath running across the middle. In the distance Evie could see a church. 'Remember how I told you that when I was a little girl we used to walk across a field to go to church?' Grandma said.

Evie nodded.

'Well, this is it. We're back in that field. And when we get to the churchyard there's something I want to show you.'

The churchyard was smaller than Evie remembered, and it didn't have as many graves in it. Of course, Grandad's grave wouldn't be here yet, or any of the other people's who had died since Grandma was little. But something was there that Evie did recognize.

'The white lady!' she gasped.

'Yes. Isn't she beautiful?'

The statue of the angel was clean and white and it was fully intact, with both its arms and two impressive marble wings stretching out from its back.

Grandma stood admiring the statue for a while, smiling to herself. 'I never thought I'd see her looking like that again.' She started to walk past the white angel towards a little gate that led into the woods behind the church. 'My favourite time of year when I was young was always the spring, when the primroses were out in the woods. Let's see if we can find some.'

They found lots of primroses and Grandma picked some and gave a bunch to Evie. 'Now,' she said, 'let's go back to the garden and have another pot of tea. But this time we'll ask the fairies to join us.'

When they had crossed the field and walked back through the archway into the garden, they found Star and Moonbeam hovering around the fruit cake. They seemed upset about something.

'I thought you said she was making a chocolate one!'

'She did! I saw her put the chocolate icing on.'

Queen Celeste was flying across the garden to join them. She was wearing a beautiful yellow dress with tiny stars sewn all over it, and her yellow shoes were sparkling. 'Are you having a nice time?' she asked Grandma and Evie.

'A wonderful time, thank you,' Grandma answered. 'We were wondering if you would like to join us for some more tea.' She smiled at Star and Moonbeam. 'I think I fancy chocolate cake as well now.' And they looked back at the picnic and found that the fruit cake had turned back into a chocolate one.

'You are very kind,' Queen Celeste said.

'There was another fairy I once knew who loved chocolate,' Grandma told them.

'Was it Buttercup?' Evie asked.

'Yes.' Grandma turned to Queen Celeste. 'Do flower fairies ever visit Dreamland?'

'Of course. They are our fairy cousins, after all. If you want her to be in your dream then she can be here directly.' She had barely finished speaking when a bright yellow speck appeared at the other side of the garden.

'Buttercup!' Grandma gasped. 'How wonderful to see you! You haven't changed a bit!'

Buttercup inspected Grandma closely and replied, '*You* have. Look at all those wrinkles.'

Evie thought that was a very rude thing for a fairy to say, but it seemed to make Grandma laugh. 'Well, I'm twice the age I was when we first met. And humans do get wrinkly when they get old – unlike fairies!'

'Is that daughter of yours wrinkly too?

The one who lost all her fairy sense.'

Grandma laughed again. 'I don't think she'd like to be called wrinkly.' She pointed to Evie. 'This is *her* daughter, who has plenty of fairy sense. Evie has a present for you and the other flower fairies, don't you, Evie?'

Evie couldn't think what Grandma meant at first. Then she remembered her doll's house, which she *still* hadn't set up at the bottom of Grandma's garden. She started to describe it to Buttercup but the fairy interrupted her.

'I've already seen it. You left your window open one night so I flew in and had a look.'

'That was *you*?'

'I was going to come out and say hello but then your mother came downstairs. Did you really bring it for us?'

Evie nodded.

'Evie, why don't you put it at the bottom of my garden tomorrow?' Grandma said. 'Then Buttercup and her friends will have plenty of time to play in it before the summer ends and it gets too cold.'

Evie promised that she would.

As they all sat drinking tea and eating cake together, Evie knew that she was going to have to leave the fairy garden soon, but she didn't know how she was going to be able to say goodbye to Grandma. To make matters worse, she was going to have to say goodbye to Star and Moonbeam and Queen Celeste as well. Now that Grandma's brass bed was no longer magical, Evie wouldn't be able to meet up with her dream-fairy friends again.

'I think you'll probably see us again, one day,' Queen Celeste replied, when Evie said what she was thinking. 'There are still a few magic beds about, you know. I'm sure if you don't lose your fairy sense, then you'll come across another one. And there's a magic bed in hospital now, thanks to you. All the patients who believe in fairies are going to get a lovely surprise.'

'Here,' Star said, handing her a tiny star-shaped hair clip just like her own. 'It's not a real star, but it will remind you of me.'

'And here's one to remind you of me,' Moonbeam said, giving her a second hair clip which was moon-shaped.

'They're beautiful. Thank you so much,' Evie said. As she took the tiny hair clips in her hand they started to sparkle.

'They do that because they've got fairy dust on them,' Moonbeam explained. 'When you get home they'll become human-sized so you can actually wear them.'

'I'll wear them lots,' Evie promised.

'Let's leave Evie to say goodbye to her grandmother now,' Queen Celeste said.

After the fairies had gone, Evie turned to face Grandma. Now that she was on her own with her for the last time, she couldn't think of anything to say.

'I'm sorry, Evie,' Grandma said softly. 'I know it's hard. Remember what I said, though. I'll always be with you in here.' She touched Evie's head very gently.

'But it won't be the same.'

'No, of course it won't. And it's going to hurt for a while. But then it will get easier, I promise.' Grandma gave Evie one last kiss. 'It's nearly morning now, my darling, so it's time for you to go.'

'But what about you, Grandma?'

'Oh, don't you worry about me. *I* don't have to go anywhere. I'm going to stay here and finish my tea.'

Evie saw that the fairies were all flying back into the garden now. The fairy who had played the lullaby in Queen Celeste's palace was with them – and she had brought her harp.

13

Evie was woken by a knock on her door. She opened her eyes and found that she was back in the big brass bed in Harry's house. It was morning.

The door opened and Mum and Dad came in.

'*Dad!*' She hadn't realized how much she'd missed him.

As Dad sat with his arm around her, Mum gently told her that Grandma had died an hour ago. They had both been with her.

'She died very peacefully, in her sleep,' Dad added.

Mum looked like she was doing her best to put on a brave face for Evie's sake, but Evie could tell that she had only just stopped crying. 'Margaret's making us some tea downstairs. Are you hungry? Do you want some breakfast?'

Evie shook her head. She still felt full from all the cake she had eaten in the middle of the night. As Evie thought of Grandma sitting drinking tea in the fairy dream garden, she wished that Mum had been able to see her like that too. Maybe then she wouldn't feel quite so bad. Perhaps if she tried to tell her about it . . .

'I had a lovely dream about Grandma,' she began.

But before she could continue, Mum was saying, 'I was just telling Dad about *my* dream. After you'd gone I dozed off again and I dreamt that Grandma was in a beautiful yellow garden drinking tea and eating cakes. She asked me to join her so I sat down beside her and we . . . well . . . we got to say all the things we wanted to say to each other.' Her eyes filled with tears. 'Dreams really are amazing things.'

'Was your head resting on Grandma's bed while you were sleeping?' Evie asked her.

'Yes. Why?'

Evie didn't reply. She couldn't help smiling. Mum must have had a bit of fairy sense left after all, so that when she'd fallen asleep on the magic bed she'd been able to visit Grandma in the dream garden too.

Dad was pointing to something on Harry's dressing table. 'Look at those. Primroses – at this time of year. I wonder where they came from.'

Evie looked over at the dressing table and saw that the bunch of primroses Grandma had picked for her was lying there. The flowers were tied together with a yellow ribbon. 'They're mine,' she said quickly.

'They're very pretty,' Mum said. 'I've always loved primroses. So did Grandma . . . Did Harry give them to you?'

Evie hesitated for a second. 'Yes,' she replied. It wasn't really a lie. After all, if Harry hadn't let her sleep in his magic bed then she couldn't have gone to Dreamland to pick the primroses with Grandma, could she?

'He's been so kind,' Mum said. 'So has Margaret. We'd better go downstairs and thank them. We'll leave you to get dressed, darling.'

Evie got dressed quickly, then went and picked up the bunch of primroses Grandma had given her. She half expected something magical to take place – for fairy dust to come shooting out of the flowers, or for each petal to suddenly start glowing in her hand. But that didn't happen. Instead, the longer she held the flowers, the more she found herself thinking how happy Grandma had been when they'd walked through the primrose woods together.

Just then there was a knock on the door. She went across and opened it. Harry was standing there.

'Well . . . ? Did you see her?' he asked softly.

Evie nodded. Her eyes were filling up. 'I can't believe I won't ever see her *again*, though.'

Harry sighed. 'I know, Evie. But I'll tell you what *I* can't believe . . . *I* can't believe your grandma actually got to visit *fairyland*. I bet that's one dream even *she* thought could never come true. But it did – thanks to you.'

Evie carried her doll's house down to the bottom of the garden that afternoon. Mum saw her doing it but she didn't say anything.

She left the last violet cream on the kitchen table inside the doll's house as a sort of house-warming gift for Buttercup.

A couple of days later, some of Grandma's friends called on Mum. Everyone was talking and drinking tea in Grandma's living room and Evie felt as if Grandma ought to be there too. She left the house and went down to the bottom of the garden where she could be on her own.

Her doll's house was still there and from the outside it didn't look any different. She didn't really expect to find any fairies inside it, but she was curious to see if the violet cream she had left was still there.

She knelt down on the ground and slid open the back to look inside. What she saw made her gasp. All the old plastic furniture was gone and in its place were the sweetest little beds and tables and chairs, all carved out of bark. All the curtains and rugs and bedcovers were made out of flower petals and the walls had been painted yellow. Miniature fairy lights were attached to the ceiling of each room and when Evie looked in the kitchen she found that it was well stocked with tiny nuts and berries and pine kernels and other fairy titbits – along with Evie's violet cream, which had been placed on a purple petal plate so that it looked like a very splendid cake.

A noise outside made her turn.

'Buttercup!' It was the first time Evie had ever seen a fairy in the daylight and she felt her heart beat quicker. Maybe she would see flower fairies quite a lot from now on. 'The house is really beautiful!'

Buttercup looked pleased. 'I'm glad you like it. I was just coming to find you. After you left the dream garden, your grandma suggested we throw a house-warming party here. She made me promise to invite you. We're having it tonight at midnight. You will come, won't you?'

Evie nodded. 'I'd love to. Especially if that's what Grandma wanted.'

'Oh, it is. She said she wanted me to make sure you had a really good time. And you will have, because flower fairies throw even better parties than dream fairies!' She laughed when she saw the doubtful look on Evie's face. 'We may not wear sparkly knickers like dream fairies do, but that doesn't stop us having just as much fun!'

Evie smiled. 'Would you like me to bring anything to the party?'

'Just a bottle of bubbly dew. Oh . . . you won't know where to find that. I tell you what – why don't you bring along a really big bar of chocolate instead?'

And as Buttercup flew off into the bushes, Evie thought that there really wasn't that much difference between dream fairies and flower fairies after all.

Fairy Dust

Gwyneth Rees

Rosie is feeling lonely after moving away to a cottage in Scotland. She misses her dad, and all her mum seems to do is work. When the lady next door tells her to watch out for fairies, Rosie can hardly believe it – until somebody starts to eat the chocolates she's been leaving out . . .

Could there really be fairies out there?

Fairy Treasure

Gwyneth Rees

When Connie is sent to stay with Aunt Alice in her boring, dusty old house, she's not very pleased. But then she meets Ruby – a book fairy!

Ruby is in trouble. She's lost an important ring and can't get back to fairyland without it.

Can Connie help Ruby find the missing ring before the doorway to fairyland is closed forever?